Night Watch

NIGHT WATCH

BY STEPHEN KOCH

Harper & Row, Publishers

New York, Evanston, and London

First HARPER PAPERBACK edition, published 1970 by Harper & Row, Publishers, Inc., New York, N.Y. 10016.

LIBRARY OF CONGRESS CATALOG CARD NUMBER: 69-15279

To answer the question, What is the Now? we
reply, for example, the Now is night-time.
To test the truth of this certainty of sense,
a simple experiment is all we need. Write
that truth down.

HEGEL, The Phenomenology of Mind

Night Watch

Part One

COME here. You are looking at a male adolescent body naked from head to pubis and laid on a surgical table, out cold. The head has flopped to one side—in its profile, the dark, gentle eyelashes are closed. The body's naked arms, the hairless chest, the abdomen and waist are all pinkish black in the lurid surgical lights, and right at the fold of the white sheet across his legs you can see the curling black mass of pubic hair, a crest above the buttocks, which are flattened by the body's reclining dead weight. This tender body is insensate. Fire a forty-five half an inch from its ear, and it won't hear a thing, won't wince. Spray its naked flesh with napalm and it won't twitch. Peel open the boy's eyelids, and the blank blue eyes will stare at you without knowing that they are staring, without flicking in their sockets, without blinking if you slap the boy's face. It's a body that can't see or feel the darkness where it has lost itself, and in a few minutes it won't feel the gleaming scalpel peel through the untouched olive skin and pare through layer after layer of white fatty tissue and muscle, won't feel the sponges sopping tiny oozing globes of blood into white gauze while the surgeon's fingers move like brown rubber-coated tentacles. The body you see is whole,

3

exposed, but the flicker of its awareness has been doused, and if this anesthetized organism is even dreaming it doesn't know that it is dreaming, or what it sees moving there.

Stand back and keep out of the way. An orderly in white pushes a stainless-steel cart spread with glittering scissors and clamps, sutures, sponges, scalpels, black electrodes for diathermy, glass syringes, all arrayed on an immaculate linen cloth. The anesthetist—that woman in the pale-green uniform over there by those bright-orange oxygen tanks—has just picked up the mask of a respirator, and (after pulling and jabbing its tangled head straps loose) she jerks it over David Fontana's unconscious face and spins the red tank valve, a watchful eye cocked on the gauge. Another orderly is pushing the electric switch that lowers that huge surgical lamp from the center of the ceiling. The lamp groans downward, moving into place and stopping three and a half feet above the table, makes the naked skin and the white linen grow brighter and brighter until they glare.

Look at David. He is unconscious, asleep, at peace. His hairless waist breathes; a sheet is draped across his thighs. His breathing is so light that it is almost imperceptible, but his light breath moves his skin so the lamp makes its highlights crawl on it: hot glistening little patches that look like something wet. Now the beam is steadied when the orderly slaps a couple of heavy clamps on the lamp into place. A nurse in a blue pin-striped uniform stoops and gently lifts David's ankle (it was dangling over the edge of the table) and adjusts his loose, yielding leg underneath the sheet (just before he lost consciousness, David got scared and started to kick. He was terrified; he had to run away; he had to get his foot free; his foot was smothering under all those sheets because the terrible long hard table had

4

turned into an endless plain where the death wind was blowing). Now another nurse dunks a fat wad of cotton in a beaker to swab some very clear, cold liquid over the base of David's abdomen, across the incision area. The volatile wetness immediately evaporates and leaves David's skin looking chemically dried, and cold. The surgeon in charge steps to the table, smoothing rubber gloves, adjusting the fingers. He bends over David's body, very near. He is chattering to three other men standing in a respectful trio behind him. He looks up. Look at his eyeglasses glinting.

All the smells are mingling with the clatter of delicate instruments, thin stainless-steel clamps and scissors and tweezers and scalpels, while the sound of the voices is urgent, whispering. There is the smell of sterilized gauze, of heated rubber, of alcohol, of linen, of plastic, of ionized stainless steel and some kind of faintly lingering gas. Listen. The surgeon has turned his back to us. He is talking out loud.

Take one last look at David's body, and let me tell you something: While all these nurses and orderlies bustle around the table, only David's quiescence really gets to me, makes me want to keep watching him, annoys me with the wish to return when I'm distracted. He is impressive, absorbing. Think of it. Look at it. Nothing can touch him, nothing reach him. Two minutes ago he was wild, *wild*, scared crazy, flipping and twisting like a fish tossed onto the dock, slammed with spasms of terror, gulping down big mouthfuls of oxygen and trying to wrench loose his arms to save himself, save himself, save himself. . . .

Look at David now. The grown male. The little boy. The human stillness. His face, body are anonymous—anesthetic makes him an object. His delicate, mask-strapped face, his

5

closed eyes, his motionless, unshivering limbs, and that still, slow, sonorous breathing under those glaring lights. Two and a half minutes ago David's flesh was feeling all the little impulses and tremors and decisions of life, and now he is just a body, the familiar organism, nothing but flesh, weight, breathing, a chest, limbs, the colored skin.

That stillness makes David seem even more alive. David's eyes are blue. Even closed, they stare. Even shut behind those thick black lashes, they want to say something. Listen to David's breath, an amplified hiss behind that respirator they've strapped to his face. Listen to the bubbling exhalation after it. Maybe some picture or dream is passing through David's mind right now, his blackened, deadened mind. Certainly his life, the anima, is still glowing in him somehow—imagine it alive in him, scattering upward toward us like the sound of his breath. Every living organism has a soul, the light of life glowing inside each body of skin and muscle, moving within the flesh the way dust moves in a shaft of sunlight. Maybe that's what's hypnotizing us, absorbing our gaze, making us stare.

David's rich. His grandfather used to own half a dozen very large—immense—aluminum-processing plants in Canada and the United States. David hasn't got friends; his sister Harriet is his only friend, as he is hers. Don't feel sorry for them, they like their solitude; they've created it, arranged it in cold blood. On street corners in Islip, Long Island, teen-aged louts with their arms draped around girls in dirty mini-skirts sneer enviously when they see the Fontana brother and sister being driven home after school in a long black Lincoln Continental limousine with thick, deep-green-tinted windows. In back, David and Harriet sulk in the green-filtered light, glad to be

6

protected by heavy glass. As it cruises through, the car never stops or slows down. They are gone as soon as they are seen.

Of course, nothing on the sheet-draped body hints at all the money, or that David and his sister have been raised in huge, high rooms, surrounded by servants and long, sloping, shrubbery-studded lawns that are cool and green and still in the afternoons. There's a big, stately fence around the Fontana estate, about half a mile from the house, but from the highway along that fence's eastern extension the house still looks immense—sixty-three rooms on three huge floors, covering the top of a hill, with red sandstone and Victorian turrets, arched heavy porticoes and huge mansards in the late-nineteenth-century style.

Look at David's face: any boy's face, with fuzz he scrapes off three times a week. David and Harriet are each other's mirrors, existing in and for each other, for themselves. They live in solitude, their mother dead, their father absent, a drunk, the only adult in their lives an equally alcoholic aunt, named Dorothy, who lives with them in the same huge house where she and her brother forty years ago were told what the world is. Dorothy disappears, the substanceless real object between the two gleaming surfaces, and so David and Harriet have nobody but themselves for company. They are indifferent to their servants, they don't give a damn even about the sweet, frigid babushka of a woman (now demoted from nursemaid to cook) who took care of them when they were children. She remains the cipher she always was when she sent the two children to each other, carrying their indifferent little unhappinesses. The offspring of ruined fools, David and Harriet have been buttoned by obedient hands into their clothing, fed by automatons. David and Harriet have taken care of themselves, taught themselves, lived only for themselves, joined in a conspiracy of silence against the other people in the world, whom they freeze out, fade out, by turning on their shriveling indifference, that look of theirs, a kind of squinting through the soul. Offspring of a dissolute generation, they have raised each other in antarctic virtue.

Look down at David's forehead. Now that he's unconscious the skin is smooth and plain; the olive smoothness seems so pure that it looks untouched, an infant's skin. When David is awake, his forehead is usually wrinkled up in some kind of puzzled expression, and you can easily imagine his tight lips slashed by harsh, invisible perpendicular lines.

Suddenly someone is talking loudly, and the heavy, padded swinging doors flop back and forth like two big wings. A nurse in one of the light-green uniforms and wearing brown rubber gloves walks toward the surgical table carrying a mass of metal clamps swaddled like a baby in a steaming white cloth, and she shakes them together as if she were shaking a bag of coins. She says something in a big voice that laughs; she glances happily over her shoulder as she sets the package down.

Step back, come away. The surgeon holds out his hand for the knife, and a nurse puts it there.

>⟞

Harriet feels nervous and stiff, and she can't get comfortable, even though she is sinking into the firm, cradling softness of the limousine's rear seat. The light around her on the seat is greenish, and the inside of the car is entirely soundless, while the world outside—the traffic-jammed expressway, all the reinforced concrete overpasses, the housing projects, and the factories—flies by darkened in the greenish light, looking like cheap Technicolor. The carpet at Harriet's feet is gray and deep and soft, and four feet in front of her there is another piece of glass, flat and closed, separating her from the front seat and the back of the chauffeur's head, which Harriet doesn't even glance at. She is watching from the window (things are passing at sixty-five miles an hour), and sometimes she presses her thumbnail against her teeth to gnaw on it a little. The nail is wet and soft.

Because Harriet isn't really looking at anything, she isn't really aware of anything happening around her. She is anxious, and the anxiety is unexpected, intense, settling over her muscles and organs like a web of itchy, sticking, acrid cobwebs and dust. Harriet shakes her head—rapidly, almost angrily; she feels the scratchy ends of her hair slap her cheeks, and she pulls some kind of pleasure out of the jerking irritable spasm, as if she wanted to clear her head by switching her hair back and forth to wipe away some kind of mental smear.

Look at the expression on Harriet's face. Her eyes are blank, and at the same time jumpy. Her mouth is twisting, as if it were trying to pull back into its natural shape. Her cheeks are pale. Harriet can't recognize anything going on inside her; she can't think about it, can't even feel it. She lifts her thumb to her mouth and bites the nail again, as her eyes narrow into a pose. *This is the pose:* Harriet seems to be squinting at something outside the window, out beyond the expressway. She looks as if she is trying to focus on something important and far away, and she is staring so intently that simple curiosity would make anybody watching her glance out and try to find what she is staring at. Harriet is not staring at anything. Without knowing her motive, Harriet is trying to divert attention from herself, trying to make everybody stop looking at her, make everybody look at something else, anything else,

9

make everybody look away from her and her fear, make them not look at her chewing her thumbnail, make them stop staring at her, stop singling her out so unfairly.

Except that she is alone.

This is what Harriet sees: She sees the smearing, flashing, vague landscape starting to change from houses—"single family dwellings"—beyond the galvanized fence along the highway into low apartment houses, each six or eight stories high and spreading across their flat lots in a sequence of mechanical right angles designed to catch the sun. Harriet sees an immense sign on top of one, written in black letters:

NOW RENTING   2   3   4½   ROOMS

Harriet closes her eyes and gently caresses her own knee. When she opens her eyes again it still is all the same, the monotonous trailing spool of the suburban landscape, gliding and tinted green. She keeps her eyes open but stops seeing. She sees a fantasy.

This is what Harriet sees: She sees David's body a carcass, hacked to bits in the hospital bed, blood drooling like saliva from the soaked sheets.

Harriet blinks.

This is what Harriet sees: She sees David very far away, sleepy, drowsy, his whole body covered with bandages, but his eyes blinking in a warm medical painless peace, smiling at his sister in the doorway, smiling very gently and then turning away without a single word. It's all right to turn away, it's all right.

The fantasy snaps off. Harriet tries to picture the room

again but fails. She can't see the sunlight draining into the white hospital room. She can't see the real flowers she sent to David yesterday, red and white and yellow and glistening in all that sunlight. Everything has disappeared in a shiver of distaste, unacknowledged distress.

Harriet shifts her weight. She has nervously turned away from the window to stare at the back of the chauffeur's head. Look at her in there, so tight. She draws her hand across her forehead. Now she seems to relax again, a little.

This is what Harriet sees: She sees her brother's face. She sees her own face, even though it is vague, half-seen—unseen. She imagines that she is trying to say something to David, though what she is saying is unclear.

This is what Harriet sees: She sees herself sitting in a green leatherette armchair right there beside David's hospital bed. She wants to get the picture clear, and she tries to picture all the hospital-like details you are supposed to picture in a hospital room (Harriet has only seen hospital rooms on television): she tries to picture the folded white screen near the head of the bed, the hanging progress chart, the white sheets, the glass of water beside the sickbed that has been standing so long that there is a crust of crystal bubbles all over the inside of the glass. But that's all. Harriet sees herself sitting there with nothing at all to say. This hospital room doesn't have any real place in her thoughts; it has never played a part in the rituals.

The rituals. You should be told about them. Part of the way David and Harriet show their love for each other is to keep out of each other's way. Some parts of their big haunted house are for being together. Other parts are for solitude. Each night, when they meet for dinner in the small dining room with its curving ship-painted mural wallpaper and its twisting crystal-hung gold sconces, they talk. Talk. Talk. Long after the maid has taken away the last dish, they sit for hours, telling everything, going over for the thousandth time the smallest details of their lives. But when they climb the stairs to the second floor they say goodnight and stop. Harriet demurely drops her eyes toward the floor and falls silent. David walks abruptly to his bedroom at the far end of the long, dark, vaulted Victorian hall.

The second floor is reserved for solitude.

And then there are the school rituals. School is a rich private institution filling three expensive antique brick buildings near Islip. In school David and Harriet never speak to each other. They talk during the morning ride over, but when they are there, not one word, not one glance—nothing is ever allowed to flicker between them, not even a hint of contact. Only the other one knows each one's rage, his hatred, the gagging terror of being where they are—that rage can't be betrayed, because David and Harriet have to keep themselves busy being nice. Always nice—it keeps people away. It is an act that excludes the audience, the fraud used to expunge and ignore every move made toward them, to stop dead every puzzled, prying expression of curiosity and suffocate any impulse a stranger might feel to speak to them, look at them, touch them. David and Harriet despise and fear everyone, and, snarling, they make everyone scatter with the waving pistol of their shyness, their sweetness, the retiring pliancy, and above all niceness. Niceness. Physical presences not so much frightening as unnoticeable.

The charade consumes every dram of energy. Only in

school do David and Harriet ever run into that alien monster, a crowd. To be sure, it is only a small crowd of wealthy, well-bred adolescents, but to the brother and sister it is an unreadable mass of subhuman foraging animals, a blasted throng of vicious, mindless eyes and mouths and chins. Anybody might step out of that throng and demolish them with anything, a smile, some slight attention.

And when David and Harriet ride home each night in the limousine they say nothing at all. They hold each other's hands. They squeeze each other's dry, tired palms. They avoid each other's eyes.

>

The heavy, low-slung car hits a bump, and with one soundless lumping movement rides through it. Harriet rocks a little in the seat; she blinks, and her fantasy is at an end. Now that David is somewhere else than at home or in school, Harriet can't remember his place in her life. He almost stops counting when she can't locate him anywhere—in the school's common room, in the algebra class, in the small dining room leaning over his plate and sulking, in the greenhouse where they used to play, on the little stairway that leads to his turret room, the room where he used to play with his plastic soldiers when he was small.

Harriet shakes her head in annoyance again, inhales a deep full breath that makes her breasts move under her blouse. By now she has acknowledged her own agitation, and at this very moment she has begun to feel something like the nausea of anger. The inside of her mouth feels very wet, and she swallows several times. She tries to think about something else, and thinking very hard she finally succeeds, even though she has difficulty keeping the new mental picture clear in her mind.

13

The anger scares her. She hates being the person she feels like, hates feeling so weak. She hates being a little girl who has to go into the city to see somebody she doesn't want to see. She loathes the pretty little girl being driven to Great Big New York to see her poor little brother sick in the awful hospital. Harriet almost pictures a trembling, double-exposed image of herself trying to twist out of a black-and-white photograph of Shirley Temple, struggling to assume the flesh-and-blood posture of the adult woman she doesn't really feel like yet. But everything breaks apart and dissolves. Everything is confused; she closes her eyes, and her wet thumb gets squeezed in her soft fist, as if she had banged her thumbnail with a hammer. She thinks she wants to cry. She wants to picture something else, but the replacement doesn't come clear in her mind; it flickers and fades, scattering shattered bits of herself across the weak, colorless screen of her mind.

✈

Stop thinking about Harriet. Look at David—he is wearing light-brown cotton trousers with thin red stripes in them, along with a button-down light-blue shirt with short sleeves. His foot—he is wearing black, soft leather loafers—is propped on his packed suitcase, and he is slouching in a hospital armchair, his chin cupped in his hand. He is sitting in his hospital room, waiting for the chauffeur to appear and drive him home. (This time Harriet won't be coming along with the driver—after that awful visit the last time she is discreetly staying home.) David stares through the open top portion of the dutch door to the room, and his eyes are open. He doesn't move. He hasn't moved for the last several minutes. Look at the voided blue eyes—the lids are blinking very slowly, like dying beached fish drinking air.

Harriet's visit. *This is what happened:* Harriet asked David how he felt. David told her he felt all right. He told her he felt a little weak.

This is what didn't happen: David didn't tell her how exhausted he felt, or about the way he kept seeing himself drained of blood, kept feeling that the juice of life was gone, and that the world had turned into something colorless, shriveled, a set of photographs, dusty, flaky, the snickering faces of somebody else's family, and boring, boring, boring. David didn't say that his body felt unregenerative, sterile, drying and breaking apart under the white muslin sheets. He didn't say that he didn't want even to stir in the bed, even to reach for the glass of water beside him, though he felt very thirsty, almost gagging.

David looks away. His open eyes are very still. He didn't tell her that he was tortured by some itchy fantasy about a filthy hand touching his skin, some alien, fingering paw, loathsome, pulling some kind consolation on him, officious, abrasive with its nauseating gentle touch—*"Oh, my poor Davy,"* it said, *"dear, dear Davy, let me touch you, let me touch you, feel better, please feel . . ."*—and he didn't tell her how afraid he was of nausea, how he felt it was about to hit all the time. He didn't say that he wanted to double over in retching agony, gagging, tearing open his sutures underneath all the hard, white, adhesive bandages wound around his middle, how he was afraid of ripping open the stiff cloth with his own hands, of letting them do it, of letting the blood and the nylon sutures clotted into it start to spill and ooze onto the sheets. He didn't tell her that he hates her, hates her in this room, hates her damned, damned, damned visit the way he would hate to be jerked out of a gentle sleep that had been filled with light dreams. He didn't tell her that the solitude of this hospital room was precious to him the way sleep is precious to a man exhausted to death, a man hatcheted down by his enervation, whose aching head has finally sunk into the pillow, whose smarting eyes have finally closed, who is at rest at last, at last, at last.

David remembers his own curled, pink hand lying limp on the white sheet. He remembers that he can't speak, and the grating minutes crawl by. Keeping quiet around Harriet is nothing new, but this silence is like sharp fingernails gouging for blood in burnt, blackened flesh, and Harriet sits looking stupid, like an alien object, an unknown animal with a gaping mouth. She is not even a homologous creature. She is just something sitting in that chair. She looks like something found.

No words, no words—nothing even polite. The weapon turns, twisted in his own hand into his own face—aphasia, their nerve gas, their death ray, afflicting him this time, shocking him and making him shudder as he sinks into it, like the hulk of a black ship slowly settling into the bottom of a green sea.

Look at them, both of them: the pale brother in the hospital bed and the sister in her prim chair. David tries to smile, to glance at her, but he gets nothing.

Harriet tries: "Dorothy told me to send you her love."

David doesn't answer.

➤

Sitting in the chair with his foot on the suitcase, David is waiting for the three chimes of the white telephone beside his bed to beckon him downstairs to the waiting limousine. Look at his eyes again—they have realized into the unresponsive

16

stare that will mark them from now on. You go blind in order not to see. David's mind has wiped everything in this room away. The deep green linoleum floor, the darkened reddish maple furniture, the big smoked-glass vase filled with Harriet's funny choice of red roses, yellow and white daisies and sprigs of green—all of them recede, recede, pull away from David until total fade-out. Right now there are nurses bustling by the door, at this very moment there is the sound of some deep, soft gongs tolling in the hall, and the gaggle of some patient's family has just hustled by, shaking a huge paper cone filled with flowers, but all of that is just what David doesn't see, the inventory of absence, the mere distractions his withdrawn senses reject and obliterate from consciousness.

David doesn't see anything at all. The absorbing preoccupation behind those blank, black-lashed eyes leaves his mind void, numb. Speak to David, and maybe he would hear your voice, but the words would get lost and break apart, like words shouted through plate glass. This morning a pretty nurse (she was wearing pale-pink lipstick) leaned into the door and said—"Hi, Buddy, how's everything going?"—and the voice seemed coming from the bottom of a canyon.

David's revery drains him. Look at his eyes; look at his hand, limp in his lap. His lips don't move at all—except just now, a little twitch, not a smile. Look at the neurotic's vacated face, his bland imitation of madness. David is staring at something behind his eyes.

This is what he sees: Harriet is standing in the darkness of the lawn, doubled over the man who is kneeling between her shaking spread legs, squirming in the moonlight that touches her skin with its flashing flesh color. David sees the cleave of

17

her naked buttocks, the trembling curve of them squeezed and kneaded in the man's dark hands while she wiggles her legs in and out like an obscene pair of swinging doors. David almost can hear her squealing, and the violent intruder buries his face again in her wet groin, trembling as he feels the damp hairs on his lips.

David winces. His face smears as he turns away in disgust. He adjusts his foot on the suitcase.

This is what David sees: He sees himself in a leather armchair in the round unused turret room on the third floor of the Islip mansion—the turret room, his retreat, his haven, still the secret hiding place it has been from the day he discovered it when he was five years old, one of the six Victorian turrets that overhang the Fontana house in front and back. Around him curl the water-stained walls with their gaping shreds of filthy, torn wallpaper. A circle of walls around his solitude, the round room where David has spent his only gratifying— but nonetheless unhappy—hours, the room where he played when a little boy, where he sulks and masturbates now. His discovery, the five-year-old's discovery that changed his little life, where he lugged his brown-stained black-and-white panda into this thrilling secrecy, undiscovered, unsuspected by others, and pulled it close to squeeze its floppy body, kissed it on each of its fat, fuzzy cheeks and then kissed its mouth, the hanging red felt tag of its tongue. . . . And then the room became a huge flatland, a battlefield where an uncountable collection of olive-drab plastic soldiers were garrisoned, thousands of American guys crouching with Tommy guns, and M.1's, some lurching forward, crazy with their brandished, dull little silver-tinted bayonets, some forever flinging hand grenades with a scream or covering their ears and cowering before the artillery blast. Companies, divisions, Grand Armies, tossed like heaps of rifle shells into four big crates David dragged up from the gardener's shop. And even now that he is seventeen they are all still there, heaped in their boxes and shoved aside. But some of the G.I.'s got left behind, out in the middle of the floor, stragglers now, mashed by the pacing of five years into green plastic powder down where bits of broken head and leg and grenade and thigh and bayonet mingle in the grime underfoot.

The turret room overhangs a small patio below, which is surrounded by a small white raked gravel footpath. You look out from the room through one huge window of curved flawless glass, and you see the vast rear lawn of the estate, the molded, clipped, English-style shrubbery, a big grove of towering narrow trees, and—way beyond—the high, spiked fence and the highway that runs along it.

And that is what David is looking at, he is looking out on that. His feet are resting on the wide, battered oak window sill. Out beyond the fence, some automobile lights are crossing along the highway.

This is what David sees: He sees the sky, which is not domed but limitless, with stars like frost crystallizing over a huge black cloth that hangs from a rod mounted somewhere at infinity. The black land behind the fence makes the headlights seem disengaged, floating, earth satellites. Nearer to us, in the grove, the leaves in the stand of locust and tulip trees are glittering in the night light. David folds his arms and slouches into the chair, and the creak of the leather under his weight is the only sound he hears in the total darkness. Think of that lawn out there, drenched in the fresh, rotten life of late-summer cool, black air. David's hypnotized eyes trace the headlights' slow path.

But there is one little sound, now that I listen—Dorothy, downstairs, wandering from room to room, drunk, listening to the stereo and its long, almost inaudible musical throbs. Just now an unnoticeable breeze has made the huge carpet of grass shimmer. And now another sound—a big, thick click.

The old door leading onto the flagstone patio below has opened and closed with a creak, and now David can hear footsteps—hear them closely—right below his turret. Harriet is walking there—David feels his body (a moment ago relaxed in his chair) stiffen, and now she appears below him (David leans forward) stepping into the light cast by all the blazing windows downstairs. Harriet's head is lowered; her arms folded; her hair rests lightly, lightly, just barely, on her shoulders. She keeps walking away from the house, and in this light David can still see her plain white blouse and simple wool plaid skirt. She looks small down there.

Look at David's expression now. His mouth is open—you can hear his breathing—and his eyes are still completely absorbed and wholly uninterested in what they see—eyes like the look of death. A false impression. Harriet is walking in a straight line toward the center of the lawn, gazing downward so steadily that she can watch the white tips of her tennis shoes pressing into the dark grass. Sometimes David notices that Harriet looks up, glancing toward the same fence he had been staring at just a moment ago; but each time Harriet looks up she immediately looks down again.

A car is passing out there, slowly, slowing, moving at a crawl while the driver cranes over his steering wheel to gawk at that terrific old house spreading all over that great big, old hill up there. Man, man, man! Take a look at that! Wow! There must be fifty rooms up there, if there's one. Man—what trees! Will you look at those trees!

By now Harriet is almost halfway to the grove. She is getting lost in the darkness, but now she looks up again, not at the highway this time. She looks toward the grove, and so David does, too. There is nothing to see, except the dark column of glittering leaves.

But Harriet isn't going to the grove. Her path leads her to the left instead, toward a small knoll (it is invisible in the darkness), and now she is there, climbing the little hillock, leaning. After she gets to the top—it is perhaps three or four feet—she stops. She folds her arms to wait. She looks at the grove. She shivers in the breeze.

Harriet is waiting for a man. She is looking at the grove, because he is hiding there, waiting to come out. Look into the mass of high trees. Do you see that moving shadow breaking loose from the darkness at the base of the tree trunks? That's him. He walks out from his sheltered hiding place and only slows down when he reaches the knoll. He is moving almost stealthily, or rather, seductively. He is not walking, but approaching.

Who in hell is he! Who! Harriet! David is scared into stone, so terrified that he can't feel his own slamming chest or the sweat dribbling like cold slime across his palms, onto the backs of his hands—can't feel his lips tightening, twisting into a grimace. *Who in hell is he? No. No. Who is he? Who?* An intruder, someone grown, dressed in—what is he dressed in? What? What? Who! Walking on the lawn as if he owned it, and Harriet waiting for him, her arms folded. She *knew* that he was coming, that's what David can't understand. David is biting his lip. His hand is pressing against the oak window sill and making it wet. His arms are trembling; they feel weak enough to shake off and flop onto the floor.

Wait a minute. Look at what David is looking at. Harriet stands calmly on the black knoll, her arms still folded and one foot slightly in front of the other. We are seeing her from the side. She turns her head and looks toward the highway, sees nothing passing there, looks back toward the knoll, and then looks again into the dark grass. Everything is still. We've stopped hearing Dorothy's stereo.

David can't guess what this is all about, but still his senses know, and he watches the way one sees a new play based on a familiar plot, a movie based on a book one has read.

This is what he sees: Harriet lets her arms drop, so the man can slip his own under hers and pull her against him, gathering her toward him the way David rolls into his pillow at night, and now the embrace is complete—the man's lips are on Harriet's shoulder, pushing into it, making her turn her head. He has her upper arm in his strong fingers (look at his fingers working at the flesh under the sweater sleeve: his wrist-watch dial glows in the dark). The man's body is at her body, pulling into her, folding into her, working at her flesh.

And now the man begins to kneel.

But his hands are fluttering and squeezing at her breasts, his lips, his cheeks are pressing into them, passing over them back and forth as on a rocking cradle, but now he squeezes against them, his arms are around her like ropes, tightening, he rolls in her breasts, his hands are moving all over them.

22

David's hand is pressing the window sill, hard. The two of them down there are tiny in the clear darkness.

The man is kneeling still more, kneeling again. In a moment his knees will touch the damp earth. Harriet's hands are on his coat sleeves, while his face presses down over her abdomen, pushing, pulling her sweater downward with it under the pressure, pressing the top of her skirt, rolling on her lower abdomen, his lips kissing, lolling in the plain wool while his hands lift to her buttocks and press again.

Harriet's hands are pulling at her skirt; David sees her hand like a tiny flesh-colored animal fluttering at her side. The kneeling man encircles Harriet's body as she stands—he is pressing her legs together, and Harriet is looking down at the top of his head. She releases her skirt and touches his hair as his head turns in her groin. She looks up, up toward the top of the grove, and now over toward the highway, and now down again, near him. Look.

Harriet has begun to pull up her skirt, jerking it up, fold by fold, through his tight embrace, which relaxes now to help her. Now all the skirt is bunched around her waist, all of it, and David can see the white smooth skin of Harriet's thigh bending outward in the light, see it shivering almost, and now see the man's smooth coat sleeve pressing into the flesh as he tightens his squeeze around her, burying his face again, pushing into her flesh, and rolling his lips against it while—now he releases her, gently—his fingers hook into the waistband of her panties, and he pulls them down below her knees in a single jabbing swoop.

David sees Harriet's naked buttocks, their trembling cleavage, and he sees the vicious, avid hands rush over it, pulling it, pulling it apart while his face forages in her groin, his face pressing the flesh and his lips rolling in the scratchy pubic hair, nuzzling against the labia. In his imagination, David can feel his sister's full, flaccid thighs pressing against the stranger's rough, bearded face in their thigh-like, tight embrace, a squeeze. Harriet is bending over her lover's head now, holding his hair, bending double, about to fall.

➤

David's hand drops from the window sill. He leans forward in the chair, his stare transfixed, dead to its own revulsion.

➤

David's fist uncurls in his lap. The open top half of the dutch door is a frame of vapid fluorescent light, and now the three chimes of the telephone ring. He looks at his watch. Ten minutes late. Ten minutes. A nurse suddenly walks by and pops her smiling face—the smile reserved for the very high-class patients—into the door, so David quickly, petulantly shuts his eyes.

➤

David has been home from the hospital for five days, and now he and Harriet are sitting opposite each other in the windowless, light-colored, muraled rich "small" dining room—a kind of suburb to the cavernous Victorian mead hall where old Grandfather Fontana used to serve the four hundred his eight-course dinners. They are waiting for the maid in her sauce-spattered white uniform to serve dinner. The paneled cherry-wood door from the long, musty, wainscoted kitchen hallway swings open, and the old woman totters in, carrying two small plates of freezing asparagus vinaigrette, the green shoots drowning in their stingingly seasoned sauce. The acidulous vinegar aroma sprays from the plates into the air before they've

24

reached the table, and the plates—light green on deep red—set up an expensive-sounding Haviland clatter when she sets them down. Harriet picks up a fork, and the smooth fibrous morsels spread apart on her tongue and the volatile flavor jumps, so intense it almost makes her start. It makes her close her eyes. The flavor pours over her tongue. She cuts loose another bite and looks up at David.

David is sitting still. When Harriet glances up at him he picks up a fork and takes some of the food himself. He puts his fork back on his plate. He lifts his elbow and leans on the table.

"Aren't you hungry, Davy?"

David doesn't reply. He can't answer Harriet as he answers the flacking, pestering questions asked by anyone else, by all the others to whom no answer can ever be allowed. With Harriet, he won't, can't, touch his big supply of mechanical banalities, silencers on a gun loaded with blanks. David can't talk, not even here in the little room where David and Harriet let themselves talk—and talk, talk, talk. The small dining room is a silent, womblike enclosure, an architectural afterthought built into the core of the house, windowless, and its walls as thick as most exterior building shells. Here, when the children are finally restored after their school ordeal, they sit eating, comforted in their solitude, and then the words break loose, slowly at first, trickling, spattering, and then coming in steady clots over the dry, sandy obstacles of their silence, and then suddenly they find themselves really talking, really talking, their talk flowing, totally unaware of itself, and by the time the maid takes away the last plate they have reached a kind of flushed, adolescent exaltation. They talk about fools and enemies, about stupid faces and what they hate; they talk about

25

their hating and how to make their hating relax; they talk about Dorothy's hung-over rages and Gemska's murky slow insolence (Gemska thinks they never notice him); they ridicule their teachers, they freeze out their nice, nice friends; they talk about hating women, about hating men, about hating the way people move and the way people talk and what they say, and Harriet, as the child of an alcoholic already embarked on her liquor phobia, talks about hating drunks, while David sits and soaks into his listening, sits there punctuating each phrase, each new turn with some strong soft word, and some change on his face, which constantly alters with sound of her voice, as if her voice were touching him. Harriet pulls her chair near his, and David leans near her, and they talk, talk, until the lights in the tomblike kitchen have been flicked off, and the rubber-soled maid pads halfway down the little corridor to the turn-off, where she turns to climb up to her rooms.

But now: "No," David answers. "I'm not really very hungry." The answer serves its function, and David pushes some asparagus with his fork. He does not smile after he speaks.

David is thinking about another scene, another set of images than this food and this stuffy, silent room, and the fragments of a nocturnal spectacle keep passing like lights across his mind, distracting him from everything, especially from the girl sitting at the other end of the table. The anticipation is almost biting his insides, almost scaring him. He keeps his fork moving politely, in a slow rhythm, putting bite after bite of the tasteless vegetable into his mouth. His eyes are smarting, but not, he imagines, from the icy acetic acid and tarragon. Chewed by the delicious pangs of expectation.

Since she sees David merely sulking over there at his plate Harriet takes the hint, shrugs inside, and keeps quiet. She eats her asparagus, slowly cutting off another forkful of the pale-green shoot and savoring it, letting the tart green taste cool her mouth (though she feels like a fool, she closes her eyes to make the taste more intense, keep it lasting longer). But it really doesn't matter if Harriet feels like a fool, since she could close her eyes, or sit on her hands tonight, without David's noticing, as she is aware. Harriet feels alone. Absolutely excluded from her brother's awareness and attention, she makes herself solitary by obliterating him from her own mind and gladly going another day without a word to, or from, him, as they have gone through so many other days. She feels uneasy about something; but she strikes that uneasiness out of her mind. She wonders about the silence, but she strikes the wondering away, as a wrinkle is flattened by a hand wiping across a sheet. Out of love, Harriet keeps quiet. She takes another bite of asparagus.

The cherry-wood door from the kitchen hallway flops again, like a blanket in the wind, and the maid comes in balancing two broad plates covered with fanning reddish slices of London broil with a pile of green Brussels sprouts, each like a tiny head of lettuce steaming under a frostlike shaved-ice covering of Parmesan, and with jagged mounds of mashed potatoes, black butter sauce pouring down their sides like flavorsome lava coursing into the valleys of tiny white mountains. On the table are goblets of water, the ice crystal in the glasses, and the glass itself a kind of ruby haze. The aromas spread around slowly, at different speeds; first Harriet smells the vegetable odor of the Brussels sprouts, the wilted hot cheese, and then she gets the familiar smell of the sliced beef beginning to rise up and drench everything.

David sulks. He hardly looks at the plate the old woman

sets in front of him. He pushes the food with his fork. Harriet is eating; she has dived in and forgotten him. She isn't looking at him, and she doesn't so much as twitch to suggest she wants to talk. David is relieved. He can be rid of this room; just take a few more bites and then go. Thank God; he doesn't want the dining room even to exist. David is imagining something else; he is imagining the still night and the mountains of stars; he imagines the unmoving grass and the thrilling, violent quietness in the air.

Look at Harriet. She gives David an indifferent glance and now sinks into eating again, feeding herself with the absorption of someone eating alone, chewing quickly, and yet seeming to ruminate, moving the fork in a regular unbroken rhythm, again and again, in one moment crunching through the London broil, cutting it without a knife, it is so tender. She chews; she vaguely turns her thoughts to her plans for tonight, and for a minute her mind does conjure up a clouded, inarticulate image; but she dismisses it with a blink as she downs a gulp of water. Now some Brussels sprouts; Harriet likes them—to her surprise, since she is always surprised by liking Brussels sprouts. This surprise does not register on her face. She takes some more. Some more potatoes, and then some more beef. Even though David is really absent during this revery, Harriet is glad that he is sitting in the room, sulky and remote though he is. She is hardly aware of him, and yet that other body sitting here in the same enclosure somehow comforts her; it keeps her from feeling lonely, and if she were factually, as well as emotionally, alone, she would be hurt and things would be boring. The food would turn banal; her appetite would go. Harriet crosses her feet under the table and scratches an ankle with her sneaker.

Look at David. His fork is moving too, but he eats utterly without relish, showing nothing—not a frown, not one narrowing of his eyes—to indicate that the Brussels sprouts taste any different from the London broil, or that either tastes different from alfalfa. His eyes have that hypnotized look you noticed first in the hospital, but now the expression is all the more vacant and cowlike because of his placid, steady swallowing.

But inside David feels a steady, shocking current of fear, a jabbing electric prod, a fearful excitement about what's coming up, and his fluttering uninterrupted anxiety is thrilling, even though the very thought of what he's going to be doing, what he wants to do, makes his mind feel tense and frayed, enervated before the fact, exhausted with the mad impulse to flee. David pictures himself wild, almost dizzy with freedom; he sees himself high, high as a kite on his own daring. *"High as a kite."* The cliché really passes through his mind and is articulated there. He recognizes the words the way you recognize a quick glimpse into the mirror.

But inside David is afraid, afraid; he hunches over his plate; the food is dry in his mouth, and when he swallows it scrapes. He is afraid of nausea; he is afraid of losing his composure in some sudden psychic accident, afraid of suddenly shoving his plate into the center of the table, afraid of snatching it up and, while the food sprays onto the chairs and walls, bashing the china against the edge of the table in shattering outrage; he is afraid of overturning the table and afraid not so much of speaking as of screaming. His tongue abrades against the dry meal that fills his mouth, and his tongue feels caught, makes him feel driven to strangulation, backed into a corner, driven against the curving wall, a wall that is crushing him in its

29

vicious embrace, even though it is the wall of his own breath.

David sets his fork on his plate. He swallows hard. He coughs. He sips from his goblet, and now Harriet glances up and smiles. With one fast swipe of his hand David lifts his napkin and swabs it across his mouth.

➤

Dinner has been over and digested for hours, and the night has settled in as if for good. David is gone; on the third floor, his turret room is empty, and the door stands open. David keeps his hiding place dark, and the burnt-out bulb in the ceiling fixture has never been replaced. More than anywhere else, David likes to sit here in his leather chair, without any light, waiting, waiting for nothing, refreshed by the blackness. The chair is still where David dragged it last, squarely in front of the big curved window. The obscurity out on the lawn is deep, almost complete: without that big sheet of curved glass shining in front of us the way it is, and reflecting the light outside, you'd never be able to tell that this room is round rather than rectangular, or that right now it happens to be empty.

Come to the window. Tonight Harriet is going to meet her boy friend out on the lawn again, and they are going to re-enact the sexual ritual David happened to witness before he went to the hospital. Except that tonight the ritual is going to be different. How different, I can't say, but somewhat so. Somebody new is involved, a stranger. I'm afraid I can't tell you what will happen. We'll have to wait and watch.

Look down to the ground right below us. As I told you, this turret happens to overhang a flagstone patio two floors down, so narrow and tightly recessed against the house that looking down from here we can't even see the edge. A sticky, jammed-up little door (never used except for this) opens onto

30

the patio from the house, and each time she leaves Harriet uses it to slip outside. Then she has to cross the patio beneath us before she pops into our field of vision. That will happen in just a moment.

By the way, Harriet's boy friend is naturally already here, hidden down there in the grove (he is smoking a cigarette), but you can be sure he won't be coming out into the open until he's good and ready, certainly not until Harriet has reached the rendezvous herself. Wait—don't even try to look for him down there in the darkness, because you'll never see him crouching under those shadowy, spiring trees. The blackness camouflages him. But when they are both out in the open, out there on the knoll, we'll see everything, and see it better than David ever did, because David never had the benefit of all this moonlight, all these stars. Look at them all! If you live in some smoggy city you can't imagine how many there are, but look up, they are the whole sky. A cloudless sky, of course, and the viridescent grass seems to roll in the scattered light while that column of trees (those tulip trees are at least 120 feet high), that column where he's waiting, shimmers upward the way a waterfall pours down, but not even down, just directionlessly, glittering leaves moving so that you can almost hear them, can't you? Remember that the grove is at least three hundred feet from where we are standing. This lawn is more like a park than a lawn, more like a vast open field, except that it has been civilized by the shrubbery and all this Victorian landscaping and the portaled fence out beyond.

By the way, if it's the knoll you're looking for, you'll never find it. Wait until Harriet starts to mark it with her body. She isn't out of doors yet, so we still have time.

Now let me explain the layout. Look over there to your

right—your far right, no, up here, near the house. Nearer, crane your neck. There. The low black outbuilding you see, the one with the peaked roof and the black shingles, looking like a miniature Swiss chalet—that's the woodworking shop, the place they use for carpentry, painting, electrical repairs, some storage, that sort of thing. But not for gardening, by the way— all that's done in the greenhouse-conservatory attached to the right wing of the house, beneath Harriet's bedroom. Anyway, even though the chalet looks pretty clear now in the moonlight, I think you'll have to look sharp to catch what I want to show you. Now, peer in toward the center of the main doorway, that one—that massive entryway of big beams overhanging the front. It may be hard to see because everything is painted black, but once you've found it look under it, carefully. Maybe you can't make it out at all until there's some action. Do you see that funny amorphous shadow under the eaves? Right. That shadow is David. You'll really see him the minute he moves, he'll stop being just a shape, and you'll see what I mean. There he is, moving, there! there! He's been waiting for the ritual to begin, but now he just shifted his weight, then leaned against the black beamed door.

Look back now, quick, right down below us. Did you hear the door open and close? Weren't you paying attention? Harriet has already crossed the patio, and now—right now— she becomes visible directly beneath us—there, you can see the top of her head. She is crossing the gravel footpath that borders the little patio, and now she's walking on the grass; she is brown hair against green and a light yellowish-orange sweater and a light, deep-blue pleated skirt that moves with her legs when she walks, and when she walks the white canvas sneakers sink into the green. (Harriet's sweater—you can still see it clearly, lit not by moonlight but by the light from the house—has a long, wispy pile that hangs loosely around her figure, her girlish figure.) Harriet's hair is loose. It lightly touches her shoulders. Her back is turned to us as she walks, of course. You cannot see her face.

➤

I want to stop this and start it all over again, from the beginning. I want to see it again, a little bit more the way I want it. That's right—step to the curved window all over again and look down. The heavy oak sash has been raised so that we can hear, as well as see, and now—pay attention this time—you hear the loud, clumsy latch of the sticky little door downstairs click and break into the creak of the opening door—absurdly, irrelevantly spooky, of course—and when Harriet closes it again she has to push against it twice, leaning her weight into it with her knee. The door is swollen and hard to close, and that's what makes that double crunching sound we heard. Now everything stays quiet while she crosses the patio in her catlike sneakers, and now there she is again in the brilliant downstairs light, illuminated in her orange and brown and blue against the white raked gravel, now against the green, passing through the winglike border as if passing out of a halo. Harriet is walking very slowly with her head down and her arms folded, her hair a young girl's hair, just gently brushing her shoulders, and her face, which we can't see, pensive, dull, her lower lips being chewed a little. She walks in a perfectly straight line in the direction of the knoll. She keeps looking at the ground, and only after she has passed into the darkness does she look up and stare for a few moments at the highway. Now she looks down again.

Notice the shop. David is standing still, nothing is moving,

33

nothing so much as jiggling down there. Now that Harriet is on the lawn, David won't so much as shift his weight. He is frozen, part of the heavy wood. The black chalet looks uninhabited, unnoticed, unseen. It is forgotten.

Look back at Harriet walking on the lawn. Her figure is lit only by moonlight, though she is walking just the way she walked before, with her head bent in that cautious, gentle way, as if she were taking advantage of this solitude to think. No; now she raises her head and looks at the highway again. A pair of headlights are passing—of course you can't hear the engine way up here. She looks down at the grass again. Even though her orange sweater seemed so bright before, all the colors on her are draining into the darkness as she gets farther from us. And yet her figure, her movements, even her pensive mood stay quite clear.

The man is late, slow on his cues; he's usually well into sight by this time. Harriet looks toward the grove, keeps looking for a few moments, and then looks down again. Hundreds of moving shadows are hiding the man—you can't see him. Wait; there he is, moving near the center of the grove. Look— *listen; listen to the leaves moving all around us, look around at the air, the night, the space.* Did you feel that breeze?— The way it passed over our faces so suddenly and began to blow through the open window, quickening like an animal waking up. The breeze is fresh, but it is slow-moving and lazy. It must have passed over the two of them out there—I mean the three of them—several moments ago. Perhaps it was as long as a minute. From this height we underestimate the distance to where they're standing out there. Harriet's arms are still folded. She looks as if she is shivering in the wind.

The man is walking slowly. He seems to be holding back.

This breeze may be slow-moving, but it's cool and gentle. It smells of the grass.

Now Harriet is at the knoll, and she leans into the little climb to the top. A bump in the middle of nowhere.

Harriet doesn't seem to mind waiting for the man. The moment she sees that he is moving toward her she turns her back to us and placidly stands there alone, gazing across the distance to the fence at the far end of the lawn. There are no cars passing on the highway. The fence is almost drowned in the silver blackness.

Harriet stands that way until the man is near her, near enough for her to hear his footsteps in the grass and the jingle of change in his pocket. Harriet hears him, she feels him near. Now she drops her arms so they flop limply to her side so that he can take hold of her now that he's on the knoll. There, he has her, he is folding himself into her and Harriet's arms still hang limp, as if she were paralyzed in his embrace.

Look at the man's head, look at the way it is turning and squirming against her that way—slowly, as if it were swimming in some kind of thick, viscous, transparent fluid. Look closely—there, for the first time you can see the side of his face. Certainly his eyes are squeezed shut. Now he turns away. His embrace across Harriet's back is almost violent and her head is thrown back and her hair hangs so that its tips brush her shoulder blades. Now she draws her head straight again, so that her cheek is rubbing and is crushed against his, and she lifts her light hands to his shoulders and feels them where they seem to move. The man is pulling his face down, against her neck, and his mouth is wide open, and he is working his curling wet lips against it while Harriet's fluttering hands keep moving on his shoulders, bouncing on them in a

35

kind of fighty recoil, as if they were painful to the touch, as if hot like steel.

And now the man begins to kneel, slowly, slowly, rolling his face, his eyes, his forehead against Harriet's breast, feeling the curling hot pile of her orange sweater gather and release as his head pulls downward. Harriet's hands still rest on his shoulders and they lower with them, and she stares forward as he moves. We can't see Harriet's eyes, but pretend she has them open, that she is gazing without looking away into the luminous grove.

The man's knees touch the ground. The grass is wet and there are pebbles in the turf. The earthy humidity immediately soaks through his light cotton trousers and his two knees feel cold. The man is close to the grass, his dampened knees sink half an inch, and he can smell it, green and wet. Harriet's hands rest lightly on his shoulders, feeling the cloth, and now she looks down again at his curling, blowing hair.

His face pushes gently into her soft abdomen, his hands pressing it toward him in the tranquilizing curl of her back, hands moving from her back down to the curve where her buttocks begin and the other, fuller skin. The man is kneeling; he looks like a kneeling man dying of thirst, trying to squeeze water out of a drenched, cold cloth. His face keeps pressing against her.

Look. The man's embrace relaxes now and Harriet lowers her hands so she can fumble with her skirt, lifting the cloth. Her legs spread apart to make a V that makes it keep riding up—look, look, you can see the curve of her thigh, firm and yet seeming to hang a little, coming into the open like a shaft of pink light. Harriet keeps bunching the cloth up until now we see her panties. He is moving his face against her, moving

36

it into her groin. Now he pulls back a little—now he pulls close into it again. He is pressing his forehead at the white cloth and his cheeks touch the bare skin of her legs.

His hands lift: he hooks his fingers into the waistband of her panties and with one unbroken slide of his forearms he jerks them down below her spreading knees, down toward her ankles, so that now he has everything, his hand sliding over the curve of her back, his closed eyes pressing into the rough flossy spray of pubic hair, the lids sensitive as if charged with marijuana, his hands holding and squeezing and lolling in the light flaccid girl buttocks, heavy fingers pressing into them until the flesh won't sink any further. The bottoms of the lobes obsess him; his fingers squeeze as he drives his face lower and now pushes upward, in toward the cunt, while Harriet's knees bend out.

Look at Harriet's head, moving back and forth the way a sparrow jumps in the gutter; look at her face moving so fast and aimlessly as she digs her fingers into his hair. Now she is looking down at him and her own hands gripping the hair; now up at the sky; now down again at his turning hanging head; now toward the fence and the empty highway, and when Harriet sees a car moving by she doesn't care. Now she looks at the grove: at its base; toward its pinnacle; above it; further above it—she is pulling her head back as if she were a starving plant trying to bend toward a source of light behind her, she seems bent double, and her hair is brushing her shoulder blades again.

The man's hands move in her buttocks, turning in a slow grind; they move into the crevice and he continues to press her groin against his face while his index finger plays across her tight sphincter, plucks it as if it were the string of an instrument. His hand is enclosed by the lobes of her buttocks, and his finger is in her anus. The rough, shaved bristles of his beard are scraping and catching in her pubic hair. Now he pulls his face still lower, pushes his lips upward, and his kiss and his tongue look for the labia. Hair curls over them and he licks the hair away. At first the little curls of flesh are rough to the tip of his tongue, but now they are smooth and wet with the human slime and they are spreading, are spreading as his face presses into her and his upper lip pushes down over the clitoris. He draws his tongue in a slow curl downward and he savors the protein urinous taste. Suddenly Harriet shrugs her head backward and she is rubbing her hands against her own loins so that the white flaccid skin seems hot against her palms and she brushes her hands against the rough wet cheeks and now she grips his hair again and pulls forward on it, now down, now leans down in the rhythm of his tongue and his pulling, hard arms as now he crumples her downward, off the knoll, behind the slope to the far side of the house and into the darkness.

>—

They're gone and we won't see them again tonight. Look at the grove over there, high, white, undisturbed, the leaves of the high locust fluttering easily in the breeze while the tulip leaves, which have rather thick, rough stems, stay firm. That's how you can tell the difference between them even at night—the moonlight glints on the locusts while the unmoving tulips seem like murky columns of dark. It's easy to distinguish each from the other, even at night. But look to your right, at the woodworking shop. The doorway is better lit now, but David's vague shadow is gone. Look, you can see the whole door. It's in the open; there's no shadow or outline of any kind against it. He's gone.

>

I'll tell you where. Just before Harriet buckled in her lover's arms and crumpled off the knoll, something like an axe chopped into David's guts and he doubled over wild with anguish and nausea, and after he doubled over he spun around, pounding the rough timber door with his slapping hands, and then he slammed his body against the door while air kept hissing through his teeth and he was making an unnamable sound in his throat. David's forehead was banging against the door and he didn't feel the pain; his hands, open flat, hit the wood again and again and again in the rhythm of the humanoid sound, which, like someone rocking himself to sleep, David was using to try to stop crying and gasping, to try to get control of his flailing arms, try to quiet his tossing insides, try to pry loose the steel band squeezing in on his breaking chest, but nothing worked, nothing was catching on, nothing was catching him, stopping him, he was losing everything, all control was going, the crazy tears were almost spraying his eyes and the acrid vomit began to slosh in his gullet, and the moment he knew his control was gone he knew he was going to throw up, too.

Then the tears really did start coming, scaring him as if he were a second person, and his hands were still hitting the wood when he felt the first stain of burning bile splash against his larynx so that he gagged. David's hands crawled on the wood, wild, weak and trembling, confused—suddenly a long black sliver from the dusty beam in the door slid into the tender skin of his palm and the instant he felt the pain he knew he couldn't control his stomach any more. He fumbled at the door knob, the hurt hand crumpled like a piece of paper, wild to get in, to get out, to get away, to hide, hide, hide. He was tugging at the door knob like a helpless baby pulling at its crib, and then David slammed into the door with all his might, and to his amazement the door gave, it swung open and he folded in after it. He lurched into the black room, and half squatting, half crawling, he clumped, banging, across the floor to the end of a big, tool-cluttered, sawdusty work-bench, afraid he would fall down because all his muscles seemed to be getting loose like untied shoelaces, and trying to hold himself upright he grabbed the edge of a big orna-mental krater that had been brought in from the garden for repairs and he held on tight. The most important thing—so he thought—was to keep standing up, but he wanted so much to fall, fall, he wanted to break in half. His throat was being sprayed with bile that sizzled like hot fat and the desperate saliva was pouring over his teeth. He felt the convulsion in his abdomen, and then he felt his gullet fill up in one strong heave and then he let the purple and white and green liquid burst from his mouth and splatter over a stinking pile of painted cover rags, heaped on the floor. Then the surge came again; a long one with lots more vomit splashing down.

It seemed over. David knelt, still leaning his weight on the urn, and coughed three times with a sound rather like the sound of sobbing. Then he suddenly hunched again while one last trickle puled out of his mouth.

It was really over now. David closed his eyes to rest. He found himself on the floor, not remembering when his body stopped standing. Then with a stab he remembered the open door, which might betray him. He tried to stand, pulling himself up by grabbing the workbench, but suddenly he was sitting again. David couldn't believe what had happened to him; he wasn't able to stand up, his knees were like water. Impossible: he couldn't be that weak. Suddenly David thought of his surgical scar and became afraid he had burst it. He groped under his shirt, feeling for any wetness on the bandages, but found them dry. He breathed. He was relieved. He pulled his hand out slowly and reaching for the workbench again to get support he hoisted himself to his feet. He still had to close the door, get it shut without a sound, without a single sound. He was terrified of any more noise, not one sound more, certain he'd already given himself away and he had to hide, hide, sink back out of sight. If he could only get to that gaping door and then drag himself back to hide in the pitch-black shop. Then he could feel safe, safe. David tried to creep on tiptoe, he tried to lift his own weight on his toes, but he couldn't, he wobbled, his wiggly ankles gave beneath him, so he had to walk, inch to the door—sometimes ten seconds' freeze between his steps—and he closed it slowly, tearing it past a honking groan in the hinge and then pushing it slowly, slowly again. Then David turned like an animal drawn to its own smell and slunk back to the workbench, the krater (a scrolled Victorian horror, *à la grec*) and the stinking rags.

David sank off his weakened legs and lay; his eyes closed out all the patches of still light spotting the black, lightless room; he touched the darkness on his tongue, against his lips; he rested his back against the urn; he rolled his hot neck against the cool concrete urn and found the room quieter than the vaulted night outside, quieter even than the turret room. David loved that silence. It helped him—silence always helped him and it helped him now. He was beginning to feel safe

41

again. The acidic stench from his vomit was beginning to spread, overwhelming the resinous, tranquilizing odor of the paint.

✕

Except for his slivered, throbbing hand—he has picked the sliver out—all David's pain is gone now, and his stomach is relieved and still. But behind his eyelids, in the darkness, the pictures from the lawn are about to come back.

Imagine David standing again in the doorway to the shop, hiding in the shadows of the gable and watching the man and the half-stripped girl twisting against each other. David can make out Harriet's face only when she looks toward the grove. Right now she is pulling up her skirt, pulling it past the kneeling man's face. David can see her round knees bending outward.

I'll tell you all this again, if necessary. David is just about to remember everything. His neck is rolling against the cool concrete of the krater. The room is black, and his eyes are blackened, closed on the darkness. He is just about to start remembering again.

"SHIT! *What the* FUCK! *It* STINKS SHIT *in here!*"

Every light in the whole place snaps on at once, flickering fluorescents making everything brighter and brighter and brighter, and as they do the same foul-mouth voice is saying softly now, to himself, "Mother fucker, some sonofabitch PUKED, barfed all over hell!" The man built around that voice is rolling on something, moving on something wooden behind David, and now something that sounds like a big plastic bowl slips off something and bounces on the floor, circling, circling, circling until it subsides into quiet. David lies perfectly still; he doesn't jump, doesn't yell, doesn't move.

The hairs on his face have bristled, and he supposes he is a little afraid. Now he opens his eyes, sits up straight, and opening his eyes to all this light immediately closes them again. But he certainly doesn't turn to see what's making all the racket.

And now a big blue-denimed, dirty, graceful twenty-two-year-old lout—big and built—slides off a large wood-and-chicken-wire dog kennel stored in the back of the shop, and stands up straight—quiet and looking around. He is wearing engineer's boots and they make some noise when he touches the floor. A white motorcycle helmet is lying still a few feet away from him. He works on the staff; his name is Dean; David has seen him perhaps a couple of times but never heard his name. When David finally looks, he'll have to think for a while before he'll remember that Dean works here. For the last hour Dean has been snoozing, stretched out on the dog kennel with his face covered Western style with his bulging motorcycle helmet and one tough knee crooked and raised, swaying a little back and forth in his sleep, while his hands lay laced on his chest like the hands of the dead in a coffin. Dean always grabs some shut-eye before his night begins, and like all deeply sensuous people he sleeps deeply even when dozing, so that it wasn't David's flailing that woke him, it was Dean's very delicate, tender sense of smell.

"Jesus Cheerist, what a fucking stink." All in a deep whisper that David can hear. "Makes me 'bout to barf."

A centipede crawls across the workbench.

Now Dean walks away from the squeaky, silenced kennel and pulls up to David, who is still sitting, almost laid out motionless, on the floor at the end of the workbench.

With one effortless unbroken graceless movement of his

43

fingers Dean flicks his long black-brown hair out of his eyes and looks down on the wreckage, and the boy, and the puke. He blinks.

"Say friend, you O. K.?"

David doesn't reply. He keeps his eyes closed.

"Hey, look, buddy, uh, you look sick and I don' wanna sound rough but just where the fuck . . . I mean like just who the he—" but with a gag Dean suddenly shuts up and catches himself fast and closes his big mouth because he has just caught on with a snap as to who "buddy" really is. Say there. Say there, man. He's never really seen David Fontana up close before. He has only caught a few glimpses, almost by accident, David out in front of the house under a portico, a couple of times, climbing out of that oceanliner of a limousine they have or David trudging along the back drive, in the afternoon, carrying his schoolbooks into that palace they have, that fucking palace. Always looking mad, always with that sister, always from way far away so that he has never had a look at the kid's face once, close up.

"Man," Dean says softly. "Man o man o man. Kid, looks like you been drinkin', huh?"

"No. I have not been drinking." David pronounces these words so softly that they can barely be heard. Dean would never have caught them without seeing David's lips move, move ever so slightly. David does not look up at the person speaking to him, but he can feel the tall, heavy body near him and tell that it is looking down on him, sensing him, sizing him up, looking him over and looking at the mess.

"Well, like, pal, ya know I dunno, but I mean it sure looks like *something's* been going on."

Yes, David thinks to himself, hearing real words passing

44

through his mind like a trailing finger on his skin, *something is happening, something is going on, something is happening to me*, and with these substanceless phrases he acknowledges his situation for the first time. He still doesn't open his eyes. He still doesn't speak to this male body that is speaking to him.

"Well, uh, sir" (Dean will immediately drop this failed experiment of "sir," which sounds all wrong), "like I mean it's good to see you alive anyway, because . . . uh . . . well, like you don't look too good off, if ya want me to tell ya."

David suddenly squirms because he thinks he can't hold back his fear about all these lights one second longer. He is just about to order them shut off again, he is just about to jump up, say something to this stupid terrible intruder, he is just about to start to scream, start to cry, when everything goes off again and a firm inner admonition to silence rises and is obeyed.

"Well, anyway, lemme help you up, O.K.?" David can feel Dean bending down, he can feel Dean's breath near his face, and the big hand closes over his weakened flabby biceps. David opens his eyes and sees Dean's black eyes, sees his dark, private, knowing smile.

Imagine Dean: His head is a white-helmeted dome, and the plastic visor curves like Vistavision across his face and shields in transparency Dean's flicking eyes, his high forehead and his hard black hair. Dean guns the handle grips, spins them, squeezes them. Imagine the spinning tires peeling over asphalt like a chain saw screaming through wood—and up front the big headlight grows blinding, like a widening gunsight, and Dean is slowly leaping up the stairs, bounding up fire escapes

45

that zigzag like teeth of a saw, he is climbing thirty stories of orange concrete, the street is a ribbon below where dust is creeping and Dean is jumping four steps at a time, breathing like a girl asleep. Imagine the business section of Hempstead, where all the teen-agers hang around all night. Imagine the luncheonette, cavelike, crowded as a subway station. Imagine the taxi stand, its lights always burning: look at that fat Negro dispatcher sitting at his microphone while the battered cars drive up and leave. Look at the kids' Kustom Kars floating by you while their engines moan and shout; imagine their faces, the girls in their smeared peaked eyeshadow and the boys in their jeans. The teen-agers' cars parked in ranks of three outside the luncheonette and the neon stretches ten blocks until it trickles into the cool blackness of residential streets and big trees. Colors in night: Orange, blue, green, white, red, black, red, white, green, blue . . . colors that hiss. They flicker and fill the night air. The sky of the whole megalopolis glows and its fire swallows Hempstead, swallows Huntington, swallows Jamaica, sucks all the light of all the suburbs into its own vast dome, and twenty miles away in its center, in the City, underground, a filthy green train smashes screaming into a fluorescent subway station and the opening doors dump faceless passengers onto endlessly rising escalators that hoist their heavy bodies into a huge empty plaza where newspapers and pieces of paper, magazines, Dixie cups, paper bags roll and blow in the breeze.

Imagine Dean: The turning Long Island Expressway bends like a hand caressing your naked back, and its tributary flows into the mercury-lit grid of the Hempstead streets. You cruise along and the lane markers shoot by like frozen, unmoving arrows (each one is about ten inches wide) while huge green-and-white road signs riveted to towering aluminum straws turn like a ladies' ballroom fan folding past a coquette's warming eyes. Dean's bike is almost silent sailing slowly past an abandoned factory with splintered windows and black shattered glass, and its flatulent steel banner BENGSTROM BREWERY rusted and fallen over itself, obliterated, a hulk the bike leaves behind in the darkness, angled out of the flow to be replaced by a shopping center, a low bank of fluorescent glass against a still shore of concrete. Over the parklike supermarket a glowing cob of plastic corn, twenty feet high and topped with a lighted cowlick of green plastic leaves, tilts with a hilarious leer over a parking lot—where the black air seems ionized in the oscillating current of white light. A female mannequin is holding a vacuum cleaner under a window topped by red letters SINGER at the far end of the bank of stores. Now the corner bends like a curving plastic shield, and next there are the long, straight, mercury-lit lines of the Main Street. Imagine Dean with his hands folding around the Duraplastic grips. He is straddling the big leather saddle, one black boot on the black pavement. The street lamps line the pavement like a flaring gauntlet of armed soldiers.

Imagine Dean: Dean sits still to follow with his eyes the whole long line of the darkened street, black like still, black water in a canal. Near the end of the road is a clock spire on top of the antique train station, the frozen hands looking as if they were bent apart by a giant into an interval always the same but always at different hours: 12:25—1:30—2:35—3:40—the time is lost or still, the real interval unchanging. Dean's hands rest on the handlebars, close over the handle grips in a delicate vio-

lence the way a man's hand closes around a woman's arm.
There is a car slowly pulling away from the luncheonette, its
lights on, and now it turns out of sight. The two barks of
sound, then the leaning, then the scream of peeling wheels like
a squealing dog and the streak of rubber slapped down on the
pavement. Dean's big hands fondle the grips the way fingers
rest on piano keys. Everywhere every head turns. Every ear
hears. Everybody gets tense and feels something inside start to
come alive and then cringe away again. Every body except
Dean's body, which is calm. Behind the racing curved visor
the air is very still and Dean's flesh grows soft and gentle
while around him the spinning lights compose.

➤

David stands up and with a gentle shrug of his shoulder
disengages his arm from Dean's hand and wobbles on his own
over to a broken old antique table-chair, propped irreparable
and unwanted against the opposite wall. Dean doesn't follow,
but watches from behind. He slips his hands into the back of
his dungarees.

David folds into the shaky chair and uses his hand to shield
his eyes from the white light. David seems to be trembling
all over. Dean decides to say something again, even though he
gets nothing back.

"Kid. Like maybe you need some help back up to the
house, huh?"

There are five fluorescent lights scattered helter-skelter on
the ceiling like five scattered sticks glaring, glaring.

David shakes his head, no. Very gently.

"Huh?" The grunt poses the question all over again, and
Dean shifts his weight, his hands still in his back pockets.

"No." There is a long pause. "I don't really want to go

back to the house right now. Let me sit here for a minute. I'll go back later, later, in a minute. Wait until I get my strength back some. Wait."

As he speaks, David closes his eyes. When he has finished, he opens them again. When they were closed, he saw Harriet standing on the lawn with her man. Now that they are open, he sees the floor and the white flickering light.

"O.K., man, 'cause it's not for me to say no to you."

David looks up at Dean, and Dean pulls his hands out of his pockets and crosses the room to climb back up onto his squeaking kennel, and cot. He holds his helmet under his arm and half reclines on it, half leans.

They are silent.

"Man." Dean waves his hand past his face as if he were shooing a fly. "Man, like it really stinks in here. No? I mean, uh, like . . ."

David looks at Dean again.

"Do you sleep in here very often?" David asks.

Dean's smile disappears and he hugs his helmet a little closer. He's scared. He feels found out. David doesn't think to reassure him with some remark to make plain that the family grants permission to use the chalet for naps.

But David just wants Dean to disappear. Just not be here. His boy's lips, still trembling a little, bend down at the corners. His hands fold on his lap. He wants this creature's presence extinguished; he feels him near. Still tasting the burning slime in his throat and on his tongue he can't say what he wants to say to this person. But he wants to say nothing at all. He wants him gone; he feels him quite near. Reaching with its habitual numb gesture, his mind finds and lifts out the banal phrase that will allow him to speak.

49

"Because I don't think I've ever seen you leave." David does not look at Dean when he says this.

Dean's lush mouth almost smiles, his lips move against each other, and he breathes so we can all hear it. Again he runs his big left hand through his hair.

"Yeah?" There is a little pause. "Like you been watching?"

David's consciousness dilates and closes another degree. His eyes shut again. He is annoyed, bored with his annoyance, outraged without being able to give so much as a single nod of recognition to his rage. "No, of course not." These words are spoken just below the level of audibility. Once again David is afraid about the lights, terrified, terrified he'll be seen, found out! found out! these lights have *got* to go out, got to! got to! got to! David is preparing himself to say something about it. The command has almost formed on his own lips, his thin lips.

But Dean says something first—loud, deep, slow, sneaky.

"But, uh, man . . . you've kinda been watchin' somethin', haven't you?" David looks at Dean and sees a deep secret smile, a luscious, informed private leer playing across his heavy, fine-boned face. "Like, I mean I bet there's something you really been watching hard, huh, kid? Close. Real, real close?"

>

Imagine Dean: Imagine Dean standing naked, rocking on his naked, light-brown hairy buttocks, rocking against an antique marble dressing table, his big legs and classic torso evenly tanned without even the swim suit of white skin left in between. You can see his whole body; you can see his whole even, smooth, olive-skinned brow when he pulls his hair back, stretching his arms, pulling his sides, his whole body tightening, his biceps filling. While he pulls he keeps his cold eye on the old woman, floundering around fat and naked over there in the bed.

"Dean. Dean." Her old eyes sag and seem wild. "Listen. Did you really close that door and lock it up?"

Dean glances toward the lofty carved mahogany door with a reassuring flick of his eyes. He smiles with one corner of his mouth. He keeps watching the woman move.

"Well, O.K. then, O.K., that's all right then." The old woman is muttering. A new idea. She stops. "*You* young ones really know how," and she laughs, leering, smirking. "You really, really do seem to know how. *That* I've got to hand to you, you really do."

The old woman is staring. "You bastard, you really did gimme a run for the money, you . . . you . . ." She stops at the word. She can't take her eyes off him. She reaches, lights a cigarette, replaces the lighter without looking away. Her movements seem learned in the movies.

"And now, Dean sweetie, do something, I want you to go and pour me a drink. I want you to take one for yourself, too, if you want to, and I'm going to watch you get it." The old woman's eyes are staring, soaking; but when they move they are filled with terror. She sees crystal quarts of Scotch gurgling on the floor. She sees splintered furniture smashed and overturned. She sees nothing in this big, orderly bedroom except this male. "I'm going to watch. I'm going to watch very carefully."

A corner of Dean's mouth smirks at her staring. He rocks his weight again against the cool marble and feels it cooling him, creasing his hot skin.

Now he moves.

David freezes. The spectator knows now that he, too, has been seen. Though David had imagined that he was watching this show in a private theater, somebody else has been watching, too; somebody has been sitting in the darkness, several rows behind him. It happens that tonight the other spectator slept through the action, but only because he has seen the ballet out on the lawn so many times. Now David knows, knows; there's no point hiding it. Found out! He's been found out. Sitting on the wobbling piece of furniture, David feels that he has become transparent. He doesn't feel shame, and he doesn't even feel fear. He feels nothing, even though everything has been changed now that those spectral images of the embracing man and girl have been seen by this other guy who lies, heavy and dark, half curled up in all the predictable hackneyed apparatus of his costume—the black, buckled boots, the stretching dungarees, dirty and fitting every ripple, the wide garrison belt with brass studs and the open denim shirt, the white helmet, the hair growing that way, hanging that way—looking at David with some unreadable smile.

David is a spectator again, watching something new this time. His face loses its tension and becomes almost peaceful.

Dean decides to answer his own question, and says abruptly, "That's right, watching up real close."

He slides off the kennel and lets his helmet dangle by the chin strap he's got hooked into his right hand. Now he swings it over into his left.

"Well, anyway, this damn place sure as hell stinks now, so maybe we'd better split out, huh?"

Dean saunters to a window which opens toward the grove. The moonlight is still high, shining everywhere, but all he can see are the shimmering trees. After staring out for a few moments he turns to David, drops into contrapposto and, hooking his thumbs in his belt, brings back the dirty smile.

Dean's helmet rolls gently against his leg.

"So, man, let's clear out, waddaya say."

David assents with his silence, but he doesn't stand up yet.

"So O.K., I'll get the light." Dean walks back to the kennel, sets his helmet on the floor and hoists himself on one knee while he reaches for the level of the fuse box in the corner above. He's got to stretch for it, stretching one leg behind him for balance. He strains into something arresting. For a second while he reaches his posture is like the Florentine Niobids done after Lysippus. The room goes dark.

This darkness is David's sign to stand up, and he hears Dean's boots clump back onto the floor, and now David picks out Dean's hulking shadow, catches the turning white glint, in the darkness, of the motorcycle helmet swinging in his hand. David waits for Dean to open the door and he doesn't move until he sees his big body lolling as it stands there, outlined by the moonlight that switches on the door frame like a television screen. Dean looks over his shoulder and David gets a glimpse of his face, his features.

"*Come on,*" Dean says, "*nobody'll see.*"

➤

While David and Dean were walking in the darkness toward the house, Dean said to David that he had to go to New York, and invited David along. Dean said something about David looking low, about company making him feel better, but both of them knew that David didn't need company, and that Dean didn't really want to be company. The invitation was given and accepted for thoughtless, wordless reasons, the way nausea invites groaning, or the way a dry leaf invites wind.

"Man, I'll get that great big piece of automobile to *move*," Dean said. The thought of sitting behind the Lincoln's wheel made him avid, jumpy. He couldn't wait to see it again—all the glass panels, the tinted windows, the walnut dashboard and the carpeting thick as grass. The long black hood, the long, long black car. "Man, I'll make that piece of automobile *move!*" The boast was Dean's request for the car; David's giggle was consent, and as soon as he had it Dean coolly turned and started walking toward the garage as if he owned it, trailing David Fontana fifteen feet behind.

Nobody hears the humming electric garage door turn on and rise. Nobody hears the tuned, muted engine of the huge Continental turn, start, idle.

But when Dean gunned that great big engine and squealed down the long curving drive toward the gate, down in the grove Harriet spun her head and grabbed her naked lover's arm—terrified, terrified.

>

The two young men drove away twenty minutes ago and nobody has so much as stirred out on the back lawn since. You watched the big polished black limousine ease out of its garage with lights off, stall, and pull past the east wing of the house, toward the front drive. You saw the automatic garage door descend after the car had gone. But now there's something more to see, so come over to the curved window again. Harriet is dressed, and she's walking back to the house—alone, of course. Talk about keeping cool—there isn't a single crack in her composure; nothing on or about her could ever give her away. She's gotten close to the house and you can see the colors in her clothes again, see the way she walks. And just look at the way she walks, as if she were just stepping back after stepping out for a breath of fresh air. And her clothes—perfect, neat, orderly—not one grass stain, not one betraying, clinging little twig even, despite all that sticky mohair. Her arms are folded. She's been especially smooth about her hair: not too messy, not too neat—certainly it doesn't look freshly combed. Harriet is safe.

By the way, take a look at that pair of lights pulling along out there on the highway—just at the far corner of our field of vision. Right: it's the boy friend's car. He parks it every night practically in the ditch and then he squeezes in through a gap in the fence left by a missing spear.

Listen. Harriet has just opened the patio door and then closed it again, and for some reason this time it didn't stick. Harriet just closes it, calmly, not trying to squeeze it shut silently and not wincing when it bangs a little.

The lawn outside is empty now—dark, light, the same.

Harriet isn't going to make it to the stairs, because Dorothy has just come lurching into the hall with lots of loud talk and big smiles. The old woman is nagging her niece again to get drunk with her. "Harriet dear, I didn't know you were down here, but since you're here and since you've obviously got nothing to do, why not come in and have a little drinky with me, huh, don't you want to spend a little time with your dear old Aunt Dorothy once in a while? Huh? You got something against her?"

Or a somewhat, though not very, different tack. "Harriet sweetie, you know I've been thinking a lot about you lately and what a woman you're getting to be, and you know I think you are developing in all sorts of wonderful ways, but, sweetie, you have just *got* to drop this prudery you have about alcohol, I mean, dear, in this day and age it isn't really ladylike, so why don't you come in and keep me a little company and have a couple of cocktails, just for the social fun of it, if you know what I mean, huh?"

Or perhaps there will be the movie version of the loving, cultivated mother speaking to her own grown daughter, not condescendingly, not sentimentally, but straightforwardly, as a Lady, a peer.

"Harriet, my dear, would you care to join me for a drink?"

These taunts are a regular part of life. Like every drunk, Dorothy feels relieved when people give approval by joining her. And, like most people who spend their childhoods with serious alcoholics, both David and Harriet have a phobia about drinking. But tonight the surprise will be that Harriet says yes when Dorothy staggers out with her why-don't-you-join-me routine. She has gone into the drawing room, and she is sitting down right about now.

That's all; there's nothing more to see outside, nothing except leaves and grass. Come downstairs.

✈

Stand in the doorway of Dorothy's downstairs sitting room and look in. A minute ago the dumbfounded Dorothy padded over to her Danish modern (eight-foot-wide) liquor cabinet and now she is clinking glasses and squishing siphons. She is wearing a heavy rose damask lounging dress; she recently had it designed just like one everybody saw a thousand times in an affected perfume advertisement on television last year. Harriet is trying to look womanly (when she sits down in the deep wing chair she demurely pulls the hem of her skirt over her knees) and she is just reaching for a cigarette from the

56

round silver canister set on a mahogany end table beside her. She pulls out a cigarette, sees it is mentholated and her finger flicks through the loose ones left, looking for another brand. Finding none, she lights the one she has. Dorothy is pushing the siphon on the bottle.

Harriet says: Look at the old witch swaying over her soda bottle, that flabby carcass wrapped up in her silly wrap-around. In a second she'll swivel around and totter back here with the glasses—*I hate it*, I hate it, I hate it, but take the drink anyway, Harriet old girl, take it, sweetie pie, don't be scared, she can't hurt you, not if you keep watching, not if you keep on your guard, ready to jump. But keep on smiling, sister, smile, smile. Here she comes—let her come. In a second I'll have that drink in my hand, the cold glass will be in my fingers, touching them, and I'll watch her sit down; she'll say something to me and I'll have to say something back. O.K., O.K., I'm scared but I'm not *that* scared. I'm not *really* scared. What can she do to me, what can she do? Keep saying that. I'm scared but I'm really safe—from the outside I look perfect, perfect, nobody can guess anything about me and certainly Dorothy couldn't guess anything in a million years—so keep on smiling, sister, here she comes, so smile, smile. It's risky, but I'm getting used to risk, risk is fun, I've been practicing. Here she comes, so let's see what we can do with *her*, here she comes, let's see what can be done with dear, dumb Dorothy. Here she comes; let's see what Dorothy can do.

Harriet plasters a big friendly, girlish smile across her face while Dorothy leans over to deposit in her hand a big glass, glistening crystal brimming with bubbly Scotch and soda. Dorothy flitters little words in her raucous, sweetie voice.

"Here you go, Harriet honey—careful now, dear, it's full, just awfully full . . . you tell me now, sweetie, if Dorothy made it too watery, just too awfully watery. . . ."

Eight feet away, Dorothy settles into a low black leather couch (another TV acquisition; Dorothy saw one just like it in a TV show about a world-famous star, a violinist or actress or something; and she had the world, New York, Europe, too, all spread out at her feet) and she curls her legs under her and rather than hoist her glass and croak "Cheers" (a woman of the world, sophisticated, so sophisticated) she cringes down and pouts, huddling like a little girl getting cozy while she drinks her glass of milk before she goes off beddy bye.

Now Dorothy tries to focus on her niece. Harriet is sitting over there and she's not wearing any lipstick. Dorothy can see that at least. Dorothy can also see that Harriet is watching her without moving her eyes—she just keeps on staring at her, but her eyes look nice and she keeps smiling in that nice way that is so friendly and sweet and ready for fun. And then Harriet takes a sip from her glass, cocking her head a little, as if she were looking forward to it—Dorothy is almost amazed at how friendly Harriet is tonight. Harriet sips from her glass. Her upper lip twitches slightly in distaste, but despite her eagle-eyed attention, straining, almost squinting, Dorothy fails to observe this tiny reflex. Harriet is smiling when the glass is set back on the coaster on the end table and she awkwardly picks up the cigarette (When did Harriet start to smoke? This thought really occurs to Dorothy), and she draws on it deeply (much too deeply for someone who hates mentholated cigarettes). Harriet keeps making little movements of this kind; she seems to concentrate on making them. She is not speaking. Her gestures are all so womanly, so self-conscious, "poised."

(Even Dorothy senses something wrong, but I needn't say she hasn't a chance of catching on.) Harriet smiles. She is looking at her aunt, her stupid, drunk aunt. She waits.

"Well then," Dorothy says, "that wasn't so awfully, awfully bad, was it? Scotch and soda always makes a nice, light drink. A light drink, light. That's always the way I've always felt about it, you know, that Scotch and soda is light. I really have always felt that Scotch and soda is a woman's drink—don't you feel that? I do—it's for women, it's really a drink for us." (Harriet doesn't move and her face remains composed in two poses that flicker elusively across it—the happy little girl and the understanding friend.) "It's the soda that does it, the soda, I think, because the real thing about women is that *we* aren't willing—we just aren't *willing*—to dump a lot of sloppy poisonous, unhealthy crude oil, crude petroleum, and *acid*, into our guts just to think we're important and strong like they try to do, the men. We women don't like that sort of thing at all. That's for all the men. We women like something light. We like something that shines in the light, shines . . . like when you hold a glass up to the light, like this. . . ."

Dorothy lifts her glass and holds it in the beam of an old Tiffany turtle lamp set on a table behind the couch, and she squints through the glass at the light. This is one of her habits. Dorothy stares at the glass and the brown, fizzing drink is tinted with the colors of the rainbow. Now she draws the glass back to her lap and holds it in her hand. Again, she hunches forward on the couch, playing the little girl. Harriet says nothing.

"Well now, what have you been doing this dull summer night?"

Harriet cocks her head and pulls a gentle *moue* of wispy

boredom. "Oh, I was reading, but I got tired of it, so I decided to take a walk out on the back lawn."

"Oh, well. A walk. That's nice." Dorothy glances out an open window and sucks at her lips.

"On the back lawn, huh?" There is a pause. Then Dorothy laughs out loud. "Well, I hope you didn't stumble over any old corpses out there in the back lawn, did you, Harriet?"

"No, Dorothy, no corpses tonight." Nothing can surprise Harriet; she quickly pulls a jaunty smile.

But Dorothy's voice lowers and begins to slur: "Well, it's a spook's house anyway. Anyway, that's what your father always says, it's a spook's house—but no, that's not right. He's wrong, he's wrong. It's not a spook's house. . . ." Dorothy's voice is getting louder. "This place has plenty of things wrong with it, and I'll damn well admit it, but I'll tell you something else, what's wrong isn't spooks, oh no, not on your life, Harriet honey, it isn't spooks. Of course your father, he's free to think any damn thing he wants to about this house or me, or you—anything he wants to about any of us. Perfectly free. I don't give a damn. He doesn't like to have me living here of course, because he thinks—" Dorothy's face is getting angry— "he thinks I ought to be stumbling around with him all over Europe or some damn place, I mean living over there in Europe, just like him. Well, I can tell you this, Harriet —I can just tell you this, I'm not going to do it, that's all; I'm just not going to do it. And I can tell you another thing, Harriet —we're never going to get him back here, so don't even think about it. He's never going to come back here, and I'll tell you something else—that's fine with me. Fine. Because there's nothing wrong with this house at all, nothing except the people who live in it, and all that's changed now, so there's nothing wrong at all. Nothing at all. Myself, I'm very attached to the old place and I *always have been*." Dorothy stops short, startled by the loudness of her own voice. She lowers it, tries to make it sweet. "No, really, I'm very attached to it, deeply attached to it, and I don't find one little thing wrong with it. Not a single one. Of course, naturally, they go for that sort of thing, that helter-skelter, cling-clang kind of living, always moving around and making more trouble wherever they go, but that sort of thing isn't for *us*, it's for the *men*. We're not that way, of course, not in the least."

There is a pause.

"Will you give me a cigarette, Harriet dear? Would you mind?"

Harriet picks up the silver canister, and brings it in front of Dorothy, who doesn't look up or make a move to take it. She continues to hold her drink in both hands.

"Thank you, dear. Just set it on the floor. I'll take one when I'm ready."

Harriet sits down again in the wing chair eight feet away. Her smile makes her look as if she is going to say something.

"Actually, my walk was rather nice, Dorothy, it really was. The moonlight makes everything look really beautiful. I liked it a lot. As a matter of fact, Dorothy, you really should come along with me some night when I go out for one of my walks. I've been taking lots of walks lately, Dorothy, and you know I have to take them all alone. It'd be fun to have you come along with me to where I go—you've really just got to come some night. It's beautiful, and it would do you good."

"Who, me? Me?" Dorothy is dumbfounded. Harriet has never said anything like this to her before. Never, *never*. She

61

almost doesn't understand the words, and she wishes she hadn't heard them. She wants to be left alone.

Harriet says: The old bitch didn't expect *that*, did she? I don't suppose I've ever said anything like that to her ever before. I've spent so long learning to be politely noncommittal, just standing around, smiling, smiling, never saying a thing, never suggesting a thing, a human lamp standing here hoping Dorothy doesn't lurch into me and knock me down. I've never touched that mind of hers, never wanted to, and instead I've just been something touched, like some knickknack the drunk picks up and fondles while she wanders alone through the empty rooms, with a glass in her other hand. What am I? I'm a china figurine. Dorothy picks me up and holds me in her wobbling hand; she smiles at me with her drooling, stupid stare. Dorothy keeps holding me while she stands there weaving—I've been around for years but she looks at me as if she were surprised, as if she were seeing me for the first time. Then she looks as if she is touched, as if she feels sad—oh, so sad—and she blurts one or two gurgling imbecile words, talking to me as a little girl talks to her doll. She pulls me closer to get a better look at my little china face. Her wet stupid eyes can hardly focus, but still she wants a better look. She grips the blue, glazed folds of my peasant girl's dress. She pulls her hot, wet, shaky thumb across my painted eyes, and my painted eyes sparkle for her. And my lips—my lips smile because I know that I won't be dropped—weak, clumsy though she is, I won't be dropped. Won't be dropped, that is, only if I smile.

>

"You know, Harriet dear, there's one thing I've never been

able to understand. What in *hell* do you two kids find to do every night? I just can't understand it. I never see anyone at all around the house—*never*. I just don't understand why you don't get some of the girls from around town to come up. You must know some of the girls at school—you *must*. Wasn't that the whole idea? Wasn't it? You yourselves—both of you, David and you—you didn't want to go away to school because you both wanted to stay here. That's what you told *me*, anyway. So I really don't understand why none of the local girls are ever around here. *Nobody* is ever around here—nobody, ever, ever. The place is like a tomb; damn it, Harriet, it's like death. I just don't understand—why *not* get some of them to come up? God knows *I* don't care—and why not let them stay overnight? We've got enough bedrooms, God knows, enough for a damned army. Why, we've got bedrooms I haven't even *seen* in five years."

Harriet leans forward a little, and a fold of her hair drops from her left shoulder (some strands cling to the mohair sweater). Her mouth is straight; her eyes are warm; she seems to be thinking. She looks gentle. She looks as though she wants to explain. She looks as though she's trying to find something to say that will give her aunt peace of mind. Now she speaks, still smiling.

"We don't want friends, Dorothy. David and I don't want friends. That's all." Her smile deepens. "You see, Dorothy, we just want to stay here, alone."

>

By now the Continental limousine is on the Long Island Expressway, cruising at seventy-five miles an hour. David isn't used to sitting in the front seat. It feels funny. Dean asks where the cigarette lighter is, but David doesn't know. He fumbles on the walnut dash, pushing switches and plungers. There turn out to be two cigarette lighters. David wipes his mouth.

⤞

Harriet says: Look at the old witch's face. Now now, no undue resentments, Harriet dear, Dorothy has never really hurt you. Much. Dorothy isn't malicious. Merely helpless. Merely irrelevant. Merely destroyed. I suppose I ought to pity her, but what would pity for Dorothy turn out to be? Maybe I'd gently bend over her and gently touch her old hot forehead? Thinking about her I turn into her and look like something out of a soap opera. What's pity? Give her another drink? Take this one away, pry it out of her shaking hand? Don't make me laugh about pity—God, how tough I sound!—pity would only amaze her and make her hobble away howling, like a dying animal startled by some dumb Girl Scout in its final hiding place, curled up in the blood-stained leaves. Now now, no undue resentments, no malicious similes. Just keep old Dorothy in your mind's eye the way she is. Now Dorothy wants another drink, so she stands up and walks over to the liquor cabinet to start mixing it. She's pouring. She's seltzering. And now, ladies and gentlemen, I'm as sure as sure can be that we're going to have the melancholy stare from the window routine, with Dorothy's hand resting gently on the window frame as if she were listening to distant music. Are we really going to? Is Dorothy really going to walk over to the window and stare? Yes? Yes.

Harriet says: I remember the time before David and I discovered we could live so easily without you, without ever

64

even bothering about you. Then we were scared, afraid to come trailing like mute, wild-eyed little idiots in here to be walked over by you, Dorothy, you, big dumb Dorothy. We kept trying to come in here and then we figured things out. I learned quickly, and David took a little longer, and his learning was harsher, angrier. It made him even quieter, quieter than anyone else, Dorothy. I can remember when we used to sit on the stairs and look at the doorway of this very room and watch Anna come down the hall, carrying your dinner on a tray. I see her there now. She lifts the tray high in one hand and knocks before she opens the door. She closes it after her, and now we're alone again, David and me, only us. Just the way we want it, Dorothy, just the way we want it.

And sometimes we sat on those stairs and looked in the open door, trying to get a look at you. The room always stank to high heaven and the lights were always glaring everywhere. And sometimes we came up to the door and stood on the threshold and watched you sitting there or walking around, and we were scared you'd see us until we figured out that you never would see us, that even if you came stumbling toward us, leering, your painted eyes wide open like mouths, you still wouldn't see us. Once we decided not even to hide when you walked past the door and nothing happened; you didn't see us, of course. And once we stood there and watched you waltzing around the room, really dancing, with your whiskey glass for a partner, humming and just missing furniture all over the place until finally you stumbled face first into the sofa—and like a true drunk you didn't spill your drink, Dorothy, you didn't spill it—you just rolled over. We jumped to each side of the door, sure you would see, but of course you didn't. You never see anything, do you, Dorothy?

Harriet says: When David and I were little children we lived in a secret world, Dorothy—we lived in it then and we live in it now. It was closed to visitors, it was our own, nobody could get in because it was *ours*. This big house was alien and too large; it was filled with enemies and spies. But that didn't stop us: slowly we subdued a corner here, a corridor there, the dining room, my room, the vegetable bin in the basement, the greenhouse. The greenhouse was scariest because Bryan, the old gardener, used to always be coming in scaring us. We felt like kids caught with our hands in each other's crotches. God, how we jumped. We had our secret world, we carved it out, marked it out, established it. We wanted it that way. We preferred it. I prefer it still, Dorothy dear, still. I like it that way now, Dorothy—secret. Even now.

➤

Dorothy is talking. "Well, just the same, I just don't understand why I never see any of the other kids around here, especially now—when you're at the age when there are supposed to be kids all over. How old are you now, Harriet, anyway? Because I've never seen one of your friends around here, because you *know* I've never seen one single girl from town or from the school or someplace around here, and not one single boy for David, and why not, why *not*? I can tell you one thing, I never would have minded, absolutely not, never in a thousand years. Who was I to mind? Me, *I'm* nothing but your old Aunt Dorothy and I can tell you right here and now that you or David could always have brought anybody at all that you wanted into this house, anyone at all and I wouldn't have minded, and that goes for David too, I wouldn't even mind if he brought people . . ."

"We had our own world, Dorothy."

"Well, dear, I mean I have never really been able to understand because anybody could come up here easily, any old time. . . ."

Harriet says: Nobody could ever come up here, Dorothy, ever, anyone. This house is closed. That's just the way we happen to feel about it, and so what if I let a man come here? So what? It doesn't mean anything and it is still the way we feel about it, Dorothy, still. This house is closed. We just don't care to have visitors. They can't come. They aren't welcome. David and I have got each other, and that's plenty for us. Trespassers will be prosecuted. The magnificent Fontana estate found one mile east of Islip's village limits along Highway 7G is not open to tourists at any time. Because David and I have been very busy, Dorothy, busy being alone. Nobody's allowed. We can't be bothered, we refuse to be. Let us serve warning now: This area is occupied; the ground has been claimed. Private Property: Trespassing Forbidden. We have been watchmen, Dorothy, we have been spies. We have a warning system built, Dorothy, a DEW line, and nobody can cross our border without setting it going, setting it clanging loud—but you'll never hear it, Dorothy, it's not for you. You'll never hear any of this, but take notice. Keep off. Keep off. Keep off. Private Property. Visitors Are Forbidden. Funny, isn't it, Dorothy, we don't want to see anybody, Dorothy, I don't know why, it's just the way it is. No trespassing. TAKE NOTICE: You are entering the danger zone. All visitors are warned to protect their eyes against the blinding glare. Travel in all of the following territories by unauthorized personnel is absolutely prohibited. The failure of any unidentified craft to immediately respond or turn back will provoke instantaneous massive retaliation. Keep away, Dorothy dear, keep away. STOP. FULL STOP. ENTRY STRICTLY FORBIDDEN. DANGER. EXTREMELY HAZARDOUS ENCLOSURE. HALT. ALL TRAFFIC PROHIBITED. WARNING! WARNING! WARNING! TESTING GROUND. YOU ARE NOW ENTERING EXTREMELY DANGEROUS TERRITORY. TURN BACK, AT THE FIRST SIGN OF DISTURBANCE, TURN BACK. VISITORS TRAVEL ENTIRELY AT THEIR OWN RISK. SECURITY ENCLAVE. ANY AND ALL ENTRY STRICTLY FORBIDDEN. NO TRAFFIC WHATSOEVER. NO MOVEMENT WHATSOEVER. THIS THOROUGHFARE IS CLOSED.

>----

David lifts his arm from the back of the seat and his hand relaxes in his lap. He has been digging his fingernails into the leather seat, trying to keep sitting straight even when Dean peels through the sharp curves and makes the back tires squeal. David's back sinks lightly into the soft leather upholstery. He has eyes only for the road ahead. He is unused to sitting in the front seat of the car, but he has forgotten his unfamiliar position and sees only the undifferentiated movements on the highway, some of them streaking, some of them turning in slow, wide curves. It is as though he has entered the cone of a flickering television screen and found the tube not convex but a huge dome of falling light. The world of objects around David seems inducted into substanceless flickering space of electric charges. He isn't used to seeing Dean's hands on the wheel. He doesn't see them now. He has almost forgotten Dean,

Dean shifts his eyes toward the boy beside him. First, he sees David's limp arms, his hands folded in his lap, and then he sees David's face: it is the face of someone watching. The face is not watching him.

Dean banks his head to the side mirror and drives the accelerator down to swing the car into a passing lane. His eyebrows arch, gently. David's back is drawn into the deep-cushioned seat. Dean does not look again at David, but merely tilts his hand lightly on the top of the steering wheel. His thumb rubs gently on the serrated rim. As the car relaxes to cruising speed in the new lane, Dean suddenly jerks his foot off the accelerator and stabs it down so that the engine gasps and the car jumps on the road. Dean's face shows no change. It waits. Now he shifts his thighs on the seat and reaches toward the dash, looking for some switch. David sees his fingers fumbling tentatively on dials. The gardener's assistant is wearing perforated leather gloves, criss-crossed with leather thongs.

Dean is aware that David has turned a little, and is now looking at him.

"Let's have some music, waddaya say?"

"I don't think there's any radio."

"Huh? No music? You're kidding." Dean looks at the dashboard now and twists a likely-looking knob. A map light turns on near David's knee. He turns it off and it drops into darkness again.

"Well, it looks like you're right."

Silence again. Dean's white helmet rolls on the carpeted floor, near David's feet, but the boy is not conscious of it flopping there.

"Man, like you look whacked out of this world."

David says nothing, but continues to watch the unfamiliar

69

body hunched familiarly in the front seat. Dean has never been in this car before. He has only seen it gliding by, driven by a man in uniform. There is something peculiar about Dean's body movement, but David cannot name it.

Dean touches the wheel of the limousine as if it were that of a Porsche. Again, he banks his head to the side mirror, and glances out of it with firm, nervous eyes.

"Man, you look so whacked out, like you're whacked out of this whole world. Do you good to come to the City. You stick around that place of yours too much, that's what I think—you and your sister. Her, too. Like, you never hardly use this car, except when Gemska takes you over to that school."

Under the perforated gloves one of Dean's hands is weighted with a bulging tooled-silver ring and stone that clatters lightly on the steering wheel when he lets it spin. Dean has picked up the feel of the Lincoln, and now he wants to play. He tilts his head to the side mirror, checking for anybody pulling up on his left flank, and guns it. His tongue runs over his upper lip. He tilts his head again when the needle hits eighty; his hands are light on the wheel, and the ring is still. Dean is trying to pose like a driver at Le Mans, trying to imitate that nasty, lyric bend of the neck and shoulders when the pros ride into a curve, but it doesn't work. Like an actor without lines, he pushes the stage business, but it doesn't quite work. He tilts his head again and inches the speedometer forward a little bit more.

David watches Dean's body with absorbed, unseeing eyes, not knowing what or even how to think. David is watching Dean as a window watches sunlight.

And now Dean says something in the darkness. "Man, you should hear old Gemska talk about driving you two back

70

home from that school of yours. Gemska, that bastard, he's so full of shit. Bastard says just let him be five minutes late and, *man*, bastard says he pulls up and the two of you are just standing there waiting, just the two of you, your sister and you with your books, and you got looks in your eyes that would kill if looks could kill. Bastard says that he comes up and if looks could kill he'd just about be dead, stretched up dead on a cold marble slab, and croaked, man. Just like that, man, just like that."

Again Dean leans his head slightly to the side. He lifts a corner of his mouth, seems amused for his own sake and savors the funny feeling privately, for his private pleasure.

At first David doesn't answer him. He is watching Dean as if Dean were the show's one performer, and as if he himself were in his front-row seat, the one-man audience, not expected to say a word until life is over, to break his silence with a bravo or a Bronx cheer. But now David does speak, just as softly as he spoke back in the chalet.

"No. Gemska is wrong. It doesn't really bother us so much when he's late. But it's true we do like to get back quickly after we're through at school."

"Yeah, that's what Gemska says."

Dean also knows this: when Gemska glances into the rear-view mirror he always sees David and Harriet staring straight ahead, even though their hands are laced together. Dean also knows that two years ago David leaned forward and rolled down the window separating the driver from the passengers, to say in a voice just like the one he is using now, soft, soft, barely audible, almost choking on its own thin breath: "Drive very fast when you get to the gate, Mr. Gemska."

Dean knows that every evening the two of them tumble and

71

roll all over each other limp in the back seat, tossed by the centrifugal force of the limousine as it wildly banks between the high, vine-covered brick gateposts.

Gemska can't hear anything. The children's laughter is silent behind the thick glass.

David says: That's right, we get mad—damned mad. Mad enough to kill if silence could kill. The solitude of the school-yard is no-man's land. No: it is not even a zone of truce; it's just abandoned ground. A point on a blank map, sand land, a tract of nothing specially chosen at headquarters for that very reason, meaningless except as an outpost arbitrarily picked for the rendezvous. That's right, we don't like to be kept waiting. We watch for our man; he must be there. He's just a face, just hands on the wheel, just a foot on the accelerator, but he'd better be there. He'd better be there.

David sees this: David sees Gemska leaning on the workbench while Dean sprawls, sucking a cigarette, on the kennel. He sees Gemska roll his cigar, sees him spit. David listens to hear talk about himself and he hears in his inner ear not words but the sound of gossip, and the sound is like nectar, like a drink of something that will keep him alive—feed him, end the thirst. The two of them keep talking about him and about Harriet. David watches Dean—Dean scratches his crotch—and Dean is waiting to go to sleep so he can finish hearing Gemska talking about the Fontana kids, about him, about him.

The picture breaks apart and dies.

David says: Gemska's just a face to us. Let him do his job and keep quiet. He thinks he sees so much about us, but he's wrong, he doesn't know anything, anything. . . .

In the driver's seat, Dean still can't quite make it to feeling like a pro at Le Mans, and the failure to do it is beginning to eat into him. The tilt of his head is getting a bit shaky, and all of a sudden he feels short; his long legs wiggle under the dash, dwarfish stubs; he can hardly reach the pedals. Dean's arms seem to grope and stretch to the wheel. He feels David sitting beside him. He feels like a servant.

Dean's jaw moves and his teeth scrape. His weight jerks forward and he hits the pedal again. Now the car has turned halfway through the exit curves and the injection of new fuel makes the heavy car leap and scream.

⤐

Up above, on the highway, in the roaring cab of the diesel, a driver looks down on that fancy black car racing through the cloverleaf. "Fucking rich brats. Think they own the whole fucking road, every damn last one of the little punky bastards." The driver with big arms curls his tongue and placidly shifts his cigar to the other side of his mouth. "Let them fucking little bastards kill themselves. But not me, mister" (on the vibrating floor of the cab, fifteen Tiparillos shake in a tin box), "not me."

⤐

The cloverleaf presses David against the door. The exit isn't familiar to him. The show is about to enter a new phase, and David is beginning to be afraid of it. Now that they have come out of the long curve, they can see some of the sky-scrapers of Manhattan, off in the red and black and white electronic distance. They have almost gotten to the City, and now for the first time David wonders where Dean is taking him.

Nothing is known, nothing is the same.

There is almost no traffic to light up the filthy streets Dean is driving through now, past warehouses and brick churches that stand, black shapes without a single light, against the urban blackness. The car's tires crunch across rusting, unused trolley tracks and cobbled black pavements smeared with oil and tar. The limousine gleams where everything is dull with grime. The expression on Dean's face—lit now by the dim storefront lights, the antiquated street lamps and the expiring neon signs—has come to a peculiarly active rest. Something has clicked. Dean has decided something about something, and he's pleased with his decision; he wears it on his face. Yet wearing it this way—without a word—means it stays secret. David is watching Dean's eyes. They are looking only at the road, his lids lowered a little, expressing the new thing that is going on inside him. His leather-gloved hands rest lightly on the wheel; the leather sometimes shines in the spare, drifting lights from outside; the thin arch of his eyebrow becomes intelligent in the glow from the instrument panel. In this weird new darkness, the polished walnut of the dashboard is gleaming.

Dean has become absorbed in himself, in his driving and his destination. His will has vanished, slipped into the camouflage of perfect visibility. His consciousness, his animal awareness, has decided not to pay any more attention to the rich boy beside him. An unmoving veil, transparent as air, has been drawn between David and Dean, pulled like a magician's handkerchief out of nothing. It doesn't tremble; it won't be drawn aside; it can't be crossed. Holding his head perfectly erect, Dean is driving as if he were alone.

❧

Back at the house, Dorothy's drooling slobber has become too much even for Harriet's smooth front to withstand. She decides with a snap that this, her first experimental excursion, is over, a relative success. Sliding a kiss onto her aunt's cheek, she excuses herself (knowing that it will be hours before Dorothy manages to make it to bed) and stops for a moment, wondering if David is in his room, and then shrugs the question off and goes directly to her own bedroom.

➤

Even if he wanted to, David could never follow all these meaningless turns that Dean is making now every minute or so, each one into a street with fewer faces in a more soulless darkness, until suddenly they come to a bridge which despite its traffic seems like a ghostly relic from a forgotten century, like a rusted railroad trestle covered with gravel and weeds, crossing a depthless canyon in the Far West, miles above a tiny river below, a filament of steel and wooden beams wedged into a breach in the mountain range that has been forgotten. But beyond the angled, rusted girders of this bridge, David sees the blue-white tower of the United Nations and the cantilevered monolith: PAN AM.

The bridge pulls them into more of the nameless streets; more warehouses that seem unseen by anything human. Dean steers the black car like a pilot easing his craft over skyscrapers and elevated highways to some asphalt plain, his own secret landing field.

The spectator surrenders himself into the actor's hands. There is silence in the front seat of the Fontana limousine; even David has become aware of the silence. But now that silence is forgotten and displayed by the unbroken inner silence of David's attention, given without consciousness of any distractions at all, attention yielding itself to the dark body beside him at the wheel. As for Dean, he no longer thinks. He is seen. The car has become his own; though he is no closer to the instruments now than he had been on the highway, they respond to his touch with the delicacy of the pupil in a human eye widening in a beam of light.

Dean's body has shed its silly, thin nervousness and assumed a voluptuous opacity. The denim shirt across his chest absorbs the faint dash lights into moving patches of blue, while the same lights vanish at his chin and leave his face in darkness. His knees bend as he touches the pedal; his hands rest on the rim, spin it, straighten it, grip it, release it; and at every maneuver his eyes and their half-lowered lids remain the same and his thin eyebrows stay arched, conscious with the same mute intention. There is no one on the sidewalks. The storefronts are black. The only eyes looking are David's, and Dean doesn't see them or feel them any more.

Look at David's face. He is watching the driver. He blinks slowly, at a regular rate. His brow has the untouched look of someone very young. His mouth is closed and straight. His lips seem to be perfectly relaxed. His attention is undivided. His eyes betray no expression of any kind.

This is what they see: Dean is a painting, a piece of sculpture, except that his body moves. It turns, touches. Its eyes see. It knows itself. It commands its environment, absorbs it; everything around that body—the leather on the seat, the polished curving windshield, the black gliding buildings beyond—incline toward that presence and lose themselves in the dark capacity of its mute will. Dean is a painting, a piece of sculpture. The landscape of art is not only seen, it sees; it draws environment toward a central concern, a numinous core created in consciousness out of attention itself. Dean's body radiates darkness, and the darkness also streams in on him, beams in the mind's eye. Dean drops the shift into low, and flexes his foot against the pedal of the power brake. David's face has not moved. He does not look up to see where the car is stopping.

>-

"Wait here." Dean opens the door (a light in the front seat clicks on) and he steps out. But, before he closes the door, he bends so that David can see his dark features clearly. Dean is not smiling: "I'll be back in a little while. Half an hour, maybe. Wait here." He closes the door. The front seat is dark again.

Now David slides across the seat and looks out. Before he peers through the glass, he pushes down the hand lock.

When he looks out the window, David looks into black isolation. Dean has pulled the car into a filthy, stench-filled, narrow, lightless, lower Manhattan back street, and across the smeared, littered sidewalk he is standing with his back to the car, bending a little by a padlocked chain, which is looped through the bars of a high, black, speared metal gate. This gate is clamped across the mouth of a deep, vaulted brick arcade that runs like a tunnel through the first floor of an ancient office and factory building twelve stories high. The tunneled vault boring through the building in front of Dean is dark, darker than anything else on the street—but one yellow light bulb is burning at its extreme end, and as David's eyes adjust to the darkness, that light becomes clearer and more important. Shining from behind, it makes the chained gate black and stark. It outlines Dean's black, shifting, rippling form, a silhouette.

David glances up: scattered across the dull façade of the building are windows with their lights burning, the lights themselves dulled by being filtered through translucent sheets of polyethylene. Then there is one long dotted line drawn straight down the front of the building: red warning lights shining on each of the twelve landings on the endless stairwell.

He looks down again. Dean is standing by the gate, his fingers working and twisting at the padlock. Now it breaks loose and comes open in his hands, and the chain flops like a dead animal in his fist. Now he shoves at the gate with his heavy engineer's boot, and the rusty metal shrieks; David can hear the sound behind the closed window of the car. Now Dean slings his weight again, and there is another sound of ripping rust and steel, and now, swinging the chain in his hand with a kind of girlish lightness, Dean takes a running jump onto the crossbars and the gate swings open and he rides on it as it squeals all the way open this time.

(He closed it behind him soundlessly. He wrapped the chain and clipped the padlock.)

Now he walks through the arcade toward the burning bulb, so that as he advances deeper his swaying silhouette hardens its edges and responds to his male movements with increasing delicacy. Dean's moving outline focuses into perfect clarity just as he turns and disappears.

Look: The street is empty now. Impossible to imagine any other figures walking here; they would have to come from nowhere; have to arrive from the human world. Like the cobbled pavement, the sidewalk is smeared with tar and glitters with shattered glass. Wholly uninhabited though it is, the terrain seems like the scene of a riot or uprising; crates lie smashed, spilling filthy excelsior, the bedding of rats; near the corner— David has spotted a single street light—an overstuffed couch rots, waterlogged with rain, half its stuffing burned away, its springs ripped and bent outward, breaking with rust. The walls of the building are smeared with words written in chalk and paint: LOVE, KILL THE NIGGER BASTARDS: JUNE 12, 1967; initials; sprays of splashed paint; a chalked cross; a smear.

Still closed up in the front seat David peers out at the arcade, which seems empty now, and now he looks up again at the building's façade above it. It seems to him that there are more lights burning above than had been while Dean was still pushing at the gate, but he can't precisely locate the difference, and just as he begins to concentrate again on the building's face, he jumps; he imagines that he hears voices; he slaps his hand on the door lock; he swings his eyes to the rear window; to the left, to the right, to the front windshield. There, beneath the scarcely real light of the single street lamp he sees two Puerto Ricans laughing and scratching their sides like monkeys, lifting their fists in their eyes and forming them into mock binoculars through which they ogle the limousine, and they are laughing derisively as only poor people can.

Looking through the windshield, David can see the Puerto Ricans' lips jabber and then he thinks he can faintly hear their sneering, high-pitched voices. But the words are in Spanish, so he doesn't understand.

Something out of nowhere suddenly stabs David with a terrible fear of being afraid, of wanting to scream and run away down the street into the black intersection, insane, insane, and the thrust of his terror makes him fold over the steering wheel, bending quiet and wild away from sight of the people pestering him outside. Within this new, crumpled inside darkness, David's peace comes back. He feels better. He can sit up. It is as though a curtain had fallen for an intermission, and when David opens his eyes again he feels calm.

The two scrawny men are walking down the center of the street, away from the car, diminishing down the perspective. David watches them bow out as he might the long farewell of a TV variety act. Sometimes one of the two men stops and turns to look back at the limousine, like Jimmy Durante bidding his long, repetitious, spotlighted goodnights. David closes his eyes again.

This is what he sees: He sees Harriet bending over a man's sleeping head, breathing on his skin. She lifts his ear lobe with her tongue. She slips it between her teeth. She releases it and closes her eyes. She slides her cheek across his sleeping cheek.

This is what he hears: "Davy! Davy! Be quiet, quick! I hear the King! I hear the King! He's talking to me, Davy! Come quick, come *on!* Hurry up! Hurry up! Over here! Over here! Quick! I can hear the King! Leave the car and come here quick. There's an official message coming through from His Majesty the King!"

This is what David sees: David sees himself plunked on a red satin loveseat in the dressing room of an unused second-floor bedroom that the children have preempted to colonize as the secret headquarters for their game of Life in the Polar Wastes, or on the Tundra, or in the Desert, or (during summertime) the Jungle. The dressing room is the wasteland; the loveseat is the official car; the corner where Harriet is crouching is the sparsely furnished Quonset hut where they live and keep their meager supplies. Isolated though they are out here in the middle of nowhere, David and Harriet remain fearless servants, part missionaries, part spies, for their nameless ruler, always faithful to him. This ruler is His Majesty the King, who lives surrounded by the great in his palace far, far away. But, though His Majesty is far away, where they can never see him, the King does not forget his faithful servants. Never. He sends messages. He regularly transmits messages to them, using the huge radio transmitter specially installed on the palace roof. The electric, indeflectable beams carry the King's word around the whole world, pulsating radio waves circling the globe like circles in a pool of water, ramifying from the surface of the earth, and glowing and spreading like pain into the uninhabited blank of outer space, widening and expanding forever and ever, never stopping, until they fill the universe. But, though they go everywhere, the radio beams register only on David and Harriet's single receiver. This is the only receiver that hears. And the King's message is meant for them alone.

The message is coming through. David and Harriet listen, crouching by their tiny radio, dumbfounded with humility. And then, enlightened with the truth they have thus received, David sets out in the official car to speak to the Natives of the Rocks. Driving fearlessly in the official car, David ventures into hostile territory, among the barbaric villages, into the tiny vicious towns that are scattered like dirty clothes around the dressing room. And then, standing up on the loveseat, David delivers his speech, his performance; he does his duty for the King. He climbs up on a high speaker's platform ingeniously built onto the back end of the official car, and as his stocking feet sink in the red satin, he addresses the cringing, growling Natives of the Rocks, who are all concealed behind the bushes or trees, or else hunched mute behind the vast jagged rocks. The Natives of the Rocks are hiding everywhere, but they are completely hidden. David never sees even one. The subject of

David's address to his invisible audience is the King's message, and that message is so portentous and full that, like the Holy Name, it cannot be pronounced. Instead, David enacts the message in a kind of balletic code. Standing on the platform, trying to keep his balance on the soft cushions while Harriet watches fearfully from across the room, David waves his arms and jerks his elbows, opens and closes his fists, wets his upper lip with his tongue and scrapes his lower lip with his front teeth. He pulls at his ear like Humphrey Bogart; he sucks air between his teeth and makes a sizzling, whining sound—all in order to convey the great Message with which he has been entrusted. The natives crouch, and David knows they are lurking there, hating him. He feels their loathing even though they are invisible. And he knows that though they watch with avid anger the whole message is meaningless to them. The only thing they can understand is that the Message is coming from the King, that King whom they hold in fear, but whom they also hate, hate like death, death. Like positive and negative charges, their hatred and their fear hold them in a tingling, hypertense balance, waiting, about to spring, frozen. David's performance of the royal Message is prolonged, complex, contorted, and futile. But David doesn't care that every sign is lost, every nuance wasted, nothing of the Message known. He only cares that so far as he is concerned the information which he has received has been conveyed. For some reason it has to be conveyed, but only in silence, through gestures, before an uncomprehending audience of their enemies. Though the performance was different each time, each time the Message they received was exactly the same, and each time David and Harriet heard it coming through the crackling static it overwhelmed them both, like revelation itself.

The message David conveyed by standing on the back of the official car was that after hours and days and weeks and years, a lifetime of waiting alone, huddled over the dead receiver that emitted nothing but silence or stammering static, David and Harriet had at last heard the Voice speak again; that the beams from the great transmitter installed on the palace roof were once again pulsating around the earth, covering it. The Message that David thus conveyed was that the enemies in the capital had been routed, the traitors foiled, the sedition checked, that all was well and that, despite the treacherous contumely of all false reports, the King Is Not Dead; Repeat: The King Is Not Dead; Repeat: The King Is Not Dead; Repeat: The King Still Lives.

This is what David hears: "Davy, listen, is it really the King?"

"No, you listen, Harriet. You tell me what he says."

Harriet bends and puts her ear against the box. There is an expression of fear on her face, fear mixed with determination. She looks up.

"Davy. The King says we're supposed to steal the Crown Jewels."

David says nothing.

"Davy. They're hidden. Hidden in the Turkish City. We've got to send a spy. You can't get in the official car. You've got to go to the Turkish City and steal the Crown Jewels that are hidden there, hidden on the women's altar. They are hidden on the women's high altar in the Turkish City. The altar for women. They are hidden there in secret so nobody at all can ever see them. You've got to be a spy and go and find them there. Wait! Wait! Just a minute! The King is going to tell me their secret hiding place. Wait!"

Harriet is silent as she bends to the box again, listening, pent and troubled with the effort to hear. And now her face relaxes. The message has come through.

"Davy, come here," very softly, her voice at peace. "Now I'll whisper the secret hiding place where the King told me the Crown Jewels are hidden." She lays her hands on David's thin shoulders and brings her lips near his ear.

"Davy. This is what the King told me. The Jewels are hidden in her big green bottle of perfume."

➤

The front seat of the limousine is growing stuffy, and forgetting his terror of a minute ago, when he clamped a terrorized hand over the door lock, David pushes the button that rolls down the driver's window. The air stinks of oil, but it is cool. Near the smashed packing crates there is a rustling sound, and the excelsior is moving a little in the breeze. Now that the tinted window has been rolled down, things seem lighter. Now the light from the street lamp spreads almost through the chained gate and the dark arcade. Nobody is moving. There is nobody in the street.

David says: Dean is gone. Harriet is gone. Neither of them is near me now. I'm alone. Alone. At last. I am myself. I roll down the window and I'm not afraid. Neither of them matter to me any more. They are nothing, nothing, nothing. I turn away from them and they disappear. They leave me. What difference do they make? I shut them off. A child in a big theater sits up straight and is a little scared. A grownup slouches, walks out if he's bored.

➤

But the theater is not David's medium. The gate, the chained

84

lock, the receding, vaulted arcade in front of him are like the proscenium of a vast stage, but as such they seem archaic and tacky, unconvincing. Television is David's medium. In the years after his secret mission on the Tundra with Harriet broke down, when David watched his sister from a distance, as she watched him, television became as it were the medium of his life, partly the actual electronic screen and partly the concrete terrain that lay around him everywhere. The turret room was his television room, though there was no television set there. But it was his television room, empty and his own. No plush seats, but his own chair. No unexpected stage devices, but the unchanging screen. No fellow spectators, but solitude. And, when David left his turret room, he felt he had stepped into the indeterminate, flickering lines of a television tube, and when he saw Harriet moving down the hallway toward her room, he saw her through the electronic gray. When she turned to him her mouth smeared into vertical distortion and she was with him there, *there* behind the glass.

$\succ$

David unlocks the door of the limousine and steps into the cool, stench-ridden air. He is afraid of rats: he imagines them all around the street; he keeps his distance from the packing crates. He starts to walk toward the gate because he wants to stare into that filthy sepulchral cloister, but a dark brick wall scrawled over with yellow and white chalk stops him. People's initials and names and obscene drawings—hearts and pricks sticking up from them so the hearts turn into the design of the tightening balls and then an arrow shot through the testicles and the words I LOVE YOU lettered across the pierced scrotum. David backs away from the wall, stunned a little by the obscene scrawls, totems of the enemy. He walks to the iron gate, grips the rusty steel rods. He jiggles the links of the chain. He fingers the rusty padlock.

But now David feels a little afraid. Instead of Dean's engineer's boots he has only his preposterously delicate soft leather shoes, and his clothes feel light on his delicate skin. As he stands on this damned ground his clothes feel flimsy and effeminate, like a little boy's clothes, and his skin feels like the clear, untouched skin of a baby. David looks down at the scraped metal surface of the cold padlock resting in his child's palm, and he feels its weight, like the weight of a human organ, in his child's fingers. He drops it and turns. He feels afraid.

The street remains deserted. The mocking Puerto Rican voices have disappeared and drifted back to the real world of lights and pizzerias and groceries and people in the streets, of boys with long hair and girls with short, and men-children affecting the exotic with hanging pottery beads and granny glasses and blue denim and yellow flowers. A world which, like this one, David does not know.

Step away from David as he stands there. Step back, come up, way up; ride to the roof of this tall building and walk to the window of this high upper room. When you look down, you'll see David standing there alone, straining to picture the children's turf clanging and moaning a few blocks away (though David doesn't know it is so near) in the Village. It's a place that shrills with orange, spits and trills its red and blue music, filling the air that gurgles with the smell of sausages and spice. Blondness; black pants; flowered shirts; wide white cuffs; and neon on orange walls and streaking signs—all unknown to him except as the place where he is not. Colors are not David's light. White is his light.

Look down now, and you will see the young body standing by the gate jump suddenly. David has jumped in that startled way because he has just heard a woman's long terrified scream strike from behind one of the polyethylene windows above him. "HELP ME," she screams. "HELP ME!" she screams. "HELP ME, HELP ME, HELP ME, HELP ME, HELP ME! PLEASE, PLEASE, PLEASE!"

Stand here in the stairwell, looking down, stand in the reddish glow from the bulb burning above the landing a few feet behind us. The boy is not especially tall—five ten, maybe. His hand is gripping a spear of the gate. He is looking out into the street. The limousine not far away is a long rectangular shape of molded black steel, directly beneath us.

David was really afraid when he heard the woman scream. He is afraid still. He looks around—looking, however, toward the point from which the scream came. He is holding the spear of the gate for support now, and mutely trying to find some path inside his body through which he can direct his feelings, let them pour, let them fall, find some path to silence his fear. He decides not to go back to the car, or rather he doesn't think to flee to it.

Instead, David seems to be trying to hear some sound. One can almost hear him straining toward the silence which (since the woman across the hall shut up) is complete again. By this time he is familiar with the landscape in which he stands (look how casually, absently he caresses the rod of the gate) and in a few minutes nothing will be able to frighten him, nothing surprise him. Then let the woman scream to her heart's content. Let her even call his name if she wants to, let her whisper to him, or lick his ear.

Now let me tell you what David is going to see. Look up the dark street—peer down the whole distance, past the street light into the cross street. In the intersection you will see a building eleven stories high, narrow, tall, old. At its base you will see a brilliantly lit entryway, a complex structure of carved white stone, illuminated by hidden lights. The building you see is called either the Conduit Building or the Bayard Building (as it was originally named) or else it is left nameless—and it was designed in 1905 by Louis Sullivan. The scrollwork on that illuminated entryway is extraordinary, the best example of Sullivan's art to be seen in New York. The relief is perfect, graceful, and surprisingly (given where the place is and the extreme delicacy of the carving) it is undamaged. Not exactly the kind of thing you expect to see in a neighborhood like this, but there it is.

Now David's eye has found that lighted entryway, too, and his hand drops from the steel gate and he stands still, pondering his new discovery.

Now he begins to walk. David's posture is always stiff, even when, as now, he is alone. His hands hardly move at all with his gait. I suppose you might take his hunched look as an indication of some special fear afflicting him now, might imagine that he is moving down the street tight, ready for attack or flight. What you see is only David's habitual rigidity, which has a funny, predictable little narrow pattern. When David sits he relaxes. When he stands, he is stiff. It's no different even in the turret room.

Even down here in this black slum, Sullivan's portal to this almost abandoned Temple of Commerce is kept shining under eight or ten spotlights that make the swirling, ornamental concrete glow like something lit from within. The light on the stone is white, whiter than moonlight, whiter than the white glow of a television screen or of fluorescent tubes shining. Piling up a plastic panel of light it shines steadily, its light filtering outward into the black night air. Nobody is around. The forgotten masterpiece glows in its brilliance for nobody.

Walking steadily and slowly, David is moving toward the light, his hands hanging still and easy at his sides, and his eyes resting on the building's dulcet, narcotic allure, drawn by its whiteness, led. Something is enthralling David with some kind of gentle, lulling charm, seducing him with some feeling we can only guess by sensing the utter pacification that just now passed over him like a shadow passing over a green lawn to darken it. Something has hypnotized David; the black air around him is soothing him and the light is drawing him as it might attract insects, dopy with their narcotic craving for illumination. David is getting very near the building and the expression on his face is new. His eyes are at peace. His lips are full and still.

Now that David has come so close to the steps of the office building, he doesn't see Sullivan's lush, ingenious designs any more. He sees a Throne.

Now that he is standing within the area lit by the display lights, close enough to the entryway to touch it, he stands still and listens. David doesn't hear the humming of the lights or the sound of the distant city traffic. He hears the whining crackle of an imaginary radio.

Now that he reaches out to touch the curling leaves, the discreet Apollonian scrolled tendrils carved into the monumental entryway, David's delicate fingers reach out and jitter across the rough stone, sensitive and twitching, jumping intelligently like the fingers of a blind man passing across a page of Braille.

But David's fingers are not trying merely to trace the design curling around him now like stone life. His fingers are deciphering a language, reading words, hearing words spoken to him which he has heard before but forgotten, words which he has got to remember a thousand times again, and then again, and he remembers again like touching someone's face, touching it a new time each time even though it's perfectly remembered, entirely habitually known. David's fingers are deciphering the message he has received many times before, the Message from the King. It is frozen in the stone, perfect, flawless, alive, new, true, passing in through his fingertips right now, at this very instant, mute. And it is clear; he reads it.

And now while the air all around him hums with the steadily oscillating overtones in the perfect B-flat of ordinary alternating current, David steps into the doorway and moves to stand in the exact center of Louis Sullivan's high façade, steps onto the throne. It is glowing all around him like a vast, masterly tooled and carved nimbus, humming like an immense television screen filled with a blizzard of electronic snow, a screen into which David steps the way Alice stepped through the looking glass. David turns. He faces the filthy street. He stands still, exalted and solitary. There is nothing behind him except the slummy halls and the dusty, bankrupt offices inside. There is nothing in front of him except the street. And now the boy folds his hands.

>

Harriet has gone to her bedroom on the second floor, where she squeezes the heavy oak door shut. Her sweetly lit, serene little bedroom is at the end of a long, stained-oak corridor (David's room is at the other end), a corridor still just as dark with stately, upper-middle-class Victorian solemnity as it was when the house was built in 1885—still muted in its wine-red carpet, still lit by dim bulbs in brass sconces dripping their icicles of old crystal, still watched over by high, structured, reddish-brown stained-oak door frames.

Harriet leans against her door—like Dorothy, Harriet sometimes imitates the movies—and looks around her own peaceful, simple room. The low light comes from a softly burning lamp on her plain, Danish-modern dressing table. Harriet is looking for someplace to fall, to tumble. Her eye moves, cautiously, bewildered with her feelings, passing from object to object: the bed, a Chippendale armchair, a bench by the wall, the big, seat-wide window sill, the bed, the chair, the sill, the bed. She chooses the bed and flops, bounces, sinks. Her back relaxes, softens, and her eyes close over a comforting, swimming darkness. She feels the relief of a new stillness inside her, and calmed by the quiet privacy and her soft bed she starts to think. She lifts her arm and rests it on her forehead. She is thinking about her lover and she keeps her eyes closed. She is thinking of the hair on his chest and the hair on his soft, hard stomach. The swirl of hair around his navel. (Once he was a little boy with a round tummy like silk.) She thinks of the scratching. She thinks of his penis, turning and pushing in her, being very hard there.

Harriet lies still. She folds her hands over her abdomen.

Harriet is again trying to picture her lover's face, and again she finds she can't do it. She pushes her tongue against the membrane of her cheek. She is trying at least to pick out something—maybe his eyes, his eyebrows, his lips—something that will make the whole face come back. She tries. She tries to remember his cheek; she can almost feel it—roughness, some kind of roughness. His eyebrows, which are very dark. Some of the hairs are longer than the rest and stick out. (Just now she almost saw him. It almost came clear, but then it didn't, and everything faded out.) His eyebrows. Dark. His eyebrows. Dark, full. Harriet's tight shoulders relax in exasperation and she curtly shakes her head. "Whose *aren't*?" She has been using words to picture him, that's her mistake. "What man's eyebrows *aren't*?" This last phrase forms a real sentence in her mind. She tries again. His eyes. Nothing. His forehead. Nothing. His eyes. His eyes. His forehead. Nothing. His name. Nothing. Nothing.

Harriet gets up from the bed and walks without any purpose to the door, and now she turns to make her choice again: the bed, the chair, the window. This time she chooses to go to the window.

Looking out, the first thing she sees is the dark chalet, the woodworking shop, and then her eyes move from it to the grove, which still looks exactly as it did when we walked out of the turret room. Next Harriet looks at the invisible knoll. She locates it perfectly. And now, for no felt motive, she cranes her neck and peers through the darkness at the garage and its three closed doors.

And right now, for the first time since she was in the grove, she thinks, David—*David!* She stops short. She can't understand. David obviously has taken the car and left. How can that be? David can't drive. Gemska is home in bed, long since, and where has David gone? David never leaves. He never goes anywhere. Never. She can't understand. David is just *gone*. She cranes her neck again, quicker this time, peering down at the three doors that keep cool even though they have been found out, and their secret has been guessed.

Harriet is frowning. She turns and walks to the bedroom

door, and stops, hesitating for a moment, deciding. Then she decides. She opens the door and walks quite rapidly down the dark hall toward her brother's room. The large doorway that opens into the master bedroom—Dorothy's room—stands open, and the room is empty. Dorothy is still downstairs. Harriet glances into the big boudoir without stopping, and then sails by, really walking fast now, almost running. Seen from where we stand, she looks scared, even though we can't see her face. Harriet is scared. That girlish poise is all gone. Harriet is knocking at David's bedroom door, loud. She knocks again.

"David."

"*David.*"

"Davy?"

"David."

Move back a little from the head of the grand staircase, and look down toward the landing on the first floor. That's Dorothy you see staggering up the stairs. She has finally decided to drag her way up to bed. She's coming now. Her negligee has come open; there is a smudged whiskey glass, half full, in her hand, and she has trouble keeping her balance. She pulls on the banister, heaving her weight up step by step, except that now she loses her balance and swings out like a rudder loose from its moorings and she has to grab with both hands to save herself from falling. The glass slips from her fingers, rolls on her wrists, and the brown liquid flows over Dorothy's hands and pours to the floor in a drooling stream. She fumbles, catches it again. It is still partly full.

Look down the hall at Harriet. She's leaning against the wall at the far end of the corridor, just the way she was leaning a minute ago against her bedroom door, and rather the same way Dietrich leans on the train platform during the long closeup in *Shanghai Lily*. In a moment, Harriet's going to decide to go back to her bedroom, and she'll start coming back down the hallway, past Dorothy's open bedroom door, toward the head of the stairs. And when she gets there she's going to bump into her plastered aunt.

⤞

At this very moment Harriet's lover happens to be stepping out of his shower. He reaches for a heavy purple bath towel and begins to trundle it across his shoulders. And now he pats it on his waist, and now rubs it on his knees and over his thighs. Look at his face. It's an adult face, handsome in a rather specialized way, and with extremely intelligent eyes that are at the moment entirely unreflective. He dries his crotch and his rear end and now flicks the voluminous purple towel onto a hook. He picks up a stick of deodorant from the sink and turns to the mirror.

This is what he sees: He sees the man in the mirror with light-brown eyes and heavy eyebrows nonetheless outlined in a graceful curve, a stylized, elongated S. His nose is ordinary size; his mouth is strong and warm, without any tendency to smile. He looks rather happy. He lifts his right arm and closes his eyes. Does he look like a man in love? I can't say, I just can't say.

⤞

Dorothy is talking but her drunk, raucous voice slurs. She can hardly stand. When Harriet bumped into her at the top of the stairs she was tempted to walk by without a word until she heard her aunt say, "Well, if you're looking for your brother, he's taken off—taken off and flown away like a great

94

big jet plane, and let me tell you that it will be a Goddamned miracle if he doesn't smash up that damned car and himself and every other damned thing while he's at it, smash up everything else into little tiny bits, all splished up. So he . . . *took off*, so if you're looking he's not here, he's gone, so if you're looking for him *don't*, don't look for him any more because he's not here. Your dear sweet little brother David isn't here because he's *gone!*"

Harriet folds her arms. "Did he say where he was going?"

Dorothy's face smears in a gesture of disgust. "Don't be ridiculous. Don't be ridiculous. Of course he didn't say. Look, Harriet dear, you still have a thing or two to learn and I have a thing or two I want to tell you and I want you to take it seriously, really seriously. Of *course* he didn't say. They never say. Just tell me once when they tell you. Just once!"

Harriet answers, very quickly, "You should be going to bed, Dorothy."

This is the first time Harriet has ever spoken to her aunt using the inflection of a command.

"Oh. Oh. I see. Now I see. So I should be going to bed, should I. *I* should be going to bed? You have a thing or two to learn, little Harriet dear. *I* should be going to bed? Let me tell you something, my little child. I've *been* to bed. *You* should be doing something like that. You should be going to bed."

Harriet drops her hands and promptly begins to walk down the hall. The expression on her face is fixed. Her lips are tight.

"You! Not me! You!" Dorothy yells.

Harriet refuses to turn, and keeps walking.

There is an almost empty glass of Scotch and soda in

95

Dorothy's hand. The ice cubes are almost gone, and float like transparent insects in the diluted water.

"You! Not me! You!"

This is what Dorothy sees: She sees the naked man rocking on his buttocks against the dresser. She sees his funny smile; she sees him looking directly at someone. But Dorothy knows that she is not the person the man sees.

"You! Not me! You!"

Holding the glass in her hand, she flings her hand backward, and the liquid sprays in an arc above her, and then the glass hurtles from her hand and spins toward her niece's back.

➤

Harriet's lover steps into his pajamas. The cloth is cool against his skin, which is still hot from the shower. He lights up a cigarette, and picks up a medical journal from a coffee table beside a conventionally modernist black leather couch. There is a Navajo rug on the floor. There is a stereo set arrayed as conspicuously as possible in its electronic complexity on a spreading, stained, hard-edge walnut cabinet. There is a Miró print on the wall, unframed, behind glass. His mouth is relaxed. He draws on his cigarette.

➤

Harriet hears the whiskey glass clatter (but not break) against the wall, and sees it scuttle like a tiny glittering animal across her path.

She stops walking. She decides to turn. Dorothy is leaning against the wall, and her negligee has fallen open. Harriet feels her own rage as it works up through her body, struggling in her, moves like a blocked kinetic charge trying to reach her forehead, her eyes, her mouth, her hands. But she manages to defer her anger, hide it on the inscape of her secrecy.

Instead, a fake look of pained surprise rises to her face.

"Dorothy. You might have *hit* me."

Dorothy says nothing. She is looking at the floor.

"Sorry. I'm sorry, Harriet dear. I got excited. I didn't mean it."

"I think you've had too *much*, Dorothy."

"I think you're right. I think I'll go to sleep. I do need sleep. I'm sorry, Harriet dear. I got excited. I got excited and I didn't mean it. It's only because your brother went away and made all that noise in the driveway. All that Goddamned noise. So I think I'll go to sleep. I need sleep."

Harriet turns and walks to her bedroom, without another word, leaving Dorothy wobbling in the hall.

➤

Harriet closes the door and the first thing she sees is the bed, covered with a satin coverlet, still indented from when she lay on it before. The bed looks like safety, almost paradise. But now her exhaustion passes over her like a wave and she does not lean against the door or bump against it. Everything goes: her knees are glowing with the pain of exhaustion; her eyes feel raspy. Her arms are flimsy, flabby; they hang at her sides like an old woman's. Thin. It seems as though her breasts sag, and the skin on her face seems chafed and shriveling. Exhaustion is making Harriet feel old, and she trembles against the door. She resists the impulse to stand and drop off her clothes where she stands and then fall into the bed. Harriet looks around the empty, low-lit room.

Again, her eyes are moving across objects one by one, and

they see only what might physically support her. She sees the bed, and she blinks. The big window sill. The bench. She blinks. (Other things—pictures on the wall, the lights, the draperies at the windows, the closet doors, the bookshelf, the television set—none of them exist.) For some reason Harriet doesn't move, but stays leaning against the door, her mind empty. She looks at the bed again, at the Chippendale chair.

Harriet is exhausted, but she isn't ready to go to bed yet—though she doesn't yet know it. She is worried, frightened about David, though she doesn't know why. She hasn't decided yet what to do. In a moment she will. She is leaning against the wall, waiting for the solution to come into her mind. In a moment it will be there.

Harriet sees: She sees her bond with David. She sees their lives, united in their pact to exclude everyone else. She hears their conspiracy of silence.

Harriet sees: Harriet sees herself out in the second-floor hallway, a little girl, watching her little brother, still in short pants, walking away from her, his back turned. She sees him turn the corner into the narrow little servants' staircase that leads from the second-floor hallway to the third floor and his newly discovered turret room. Harriet's eyes are wet and smarting. She feels like she wants to cry because David said she couldn't come. Couldn't. Couldn't. The word seems incredible to her. She couldn't come. The ordinary child's solution to the ex-clusion—running to Mama—naturally doesn't even occur to her. Now she knows what it is like to be turned away, to have trust pushed in the face, to have been stopped. But the im-mediate reaction—take the story to somebody else trusted—is foreclosed. But the natural reaction is so thoroughly foreclosed that Harriet does not even *wish* for someone she could run to and tell. David is gone. She is standing in the hallway, her hands limp at her sides.

Harriet says: "I could wait up until David gets back." This is the solution. The words form a real sentence in her mind.

Harriet is still leaning against her bedroom door, staring at the uninviting bed, feeling the ache in her knees. The puzzled look on her face is somewhat cleared up since she thought of what to do, but she still doesn't move.

Harriet sees this: She sees her twelve-year-old brother hunched over his dinner plate in the dining room, morose and pulling a nasty silence. Harriet is angry with him; she wants to slap him as hard as she can. She wants to stamp her foot, again and again and again. David slops in great big nasty bites, and he's making all that noise when he eats, on purpose—of course it's on purpose. She feels like getting up and walking away. But instead she has another thought and she thinks about her breasts. She can feel them. They are there. Real. David looks like a little boy.

Harriet sees this: She sees David sauntering to the stairway that leads to the third floor. She feels left alone. She feels that she must do something about it, but she doesn't know what she can do. She walks into her own room. She goes to the window and looks down. The grove of trees is big and beautiful and the sunlight makes the lawn a great ocean of glowing, wonderful green.

➤

Once again Harriet hears the words run through her mind: "Wait up for David, that's what I'll do, I'll wait up for David, wait until he gets back." And now Harriet can move. She walks into the room and sits in the Chippendale chair, as if she intended to wait for David by sitting there until the car returned. Her legs and back relax in a wave, and she slumps back into the seat. She closes her eyes. Then she opens them again to look for a cigarette on her dressing table, but there aren't any there.

"Wait up until he's back!" This time Harriet says the sentence out loud, chiding herself, as if to say how stupid she had been not to think of it before. And now a new idea occurs to her, and she gets up and clicks out the little lamp on her dressing table. The room is dark, and she leaves it quickly, opens the door and steps back into the hall. On the way to the little stairs that lead to the third floor, she passes the empty whiskey glass that is on the floor by the baseboard, glinting.

The little set of stairs is dark and narrow, and there is no light at the top. Harriet puts out her hand and touches the banister, which is small, round, and built very close to the wall. She climbs the first five steps quite quickly, and then, because everything is entirely dark, she must test each new step with her foot before she moves forward, and her hand begins to squeeze the round wooden banister pole. As she climbs, each step is taken more slowly, and then she reaches the top—she can tell she has reached the top because her foot doesn't find another step, but only the flat floor. There is light in the third-floor hallway, moonlight coming through a skylight.

Otherwise, the third floor is dark. Harriet only vaguely remembers where David's turret room is, but without thinking she correctly turns to her left and takes fifteen hesitant steps to its doorway. She turns. She turns. This door is the only one open that she has passed so far. Harriet looks in and she can see the moonlight filling the big window. On the threshold she stops and puts out her hand, feeling for the light switch. She can't find it; there's nothing but smooth wall. She stands still instead until her night vision clears. Now she can see the curving pane of glass. Now she can make out the chair. Now she feels free to move without feeling her way.

David's armchair is just where it was when we left the room, pulled away from the window. Harriet walks to it, bends over and pushes it with her knees in its back until it is positioned directly in front of the window, and when it is there, regally overlooking the array below, she sits. The moon is almost down. The lawn is in darkness. The chalet can hardly be seen. The garage is only a black shape. The grove is a geyser of blackness, and a pair of headlights are passing, very slowly, behind.

➤

Think about David again, who is leaning against one side of Louis Sullivan's great portal, dazed, wrapped in a cloud of light. David has moved away from the center of the entryway to the wall, and he is leaning on the scrolled carved concrete, alone, weary, stunned, as if after a debauch. The scrollwork feels like the broken krater in the chalet, and David trembles a little after the delicate flushing of feelings that have left him blandly aware of his solitude, which is a solitude rather like that of someone waking up alone in a sunlit room. The streets are streets again, and the slum has come back, unthreatening. Suddenly, David is strangly conscious of his legs; he bends and feels their sides, rubbing his fingers against them.

Obviously, David has no idea of how silly he looks, standing there in a halo, testing his legs to make sure they are there. I have no idea how you feel about the matter, but for myself I was briefly quite pleased with the solitary ballet he has just enacted. I might even say I was almost absorbed in its slow unfolding. But just take a look at him out there now. A teenaged boy in an empty street, looking around as if dazed, an animal regaining its awareness of its body after being stunned by a violent electric jolt, prostrated by a drug. Except that David's collapse was delicate and slow, like fish scales scattering and drifting in the still water of an aquarium, slowly glittering along their way down to the bottom. They cloud the liquid. And, along with the scales, little strings of torn flesh are sinking.

Look at him out there. He jumps off the steps with a little hop and now he is walking back to the car, but no longer afflicted with the stiff hobble he was using before. His gait is now an easy, smooth, boy's lope, as strange in his large body as his earlier way of walking, crouching erect.

David looks comfortable on the street. He zigzags across the black-blue pavement in sharply pointed V's, and his arms are loose at his sides. Behind him, the Sullivan façade is still gleaming.

Stand here in this dark doorway, and look over at the gate, the arcade, and the limousine across the street. The single light bulb in the back of the arcade is still shining; it draws the sharp jagged teeth of the gate like charcoal lines drawn on dirty paper. In front of the gate (his legs are blocked by the hood of the Continental) you can see Dean, standing still, waiting for David to come back. Everything is quiet.

Dean is peering out into the dark street, but he can't see anything, and so he can't tell that David is already walking back to the car, oblivious of the fact that Dean has already come back onto the street from inside that big building behind him.

David is not aware of how long—how many minutes—he was standing under the Sullivan façade, and his sense of time is still loose, floating, drifting. Everything is dark around him and he moves through the black medium of the air like a fish that is gently, purposelessly wafting itself in this direction, that direction, more or less toward the car and his waiting companion. David is obscure in the darkness; he is a moving column of thicker black, and his movements out in the middle of the street are like the movements of a transparent organism across the gleaming field of light in the eye of a microscope. But he is drawing closer to the destination now, and in a minute Dean and the woman with him will recognize him moving out here—a human form.

Look: Now you can see that there are two people waiting for David—Dean and a woman. You can see her now. She has just taken Dean's arm and she is leaning against him, squeezing herself against his side. She is wearing a very short cream-colored party dress that flutters above her knees when her legs move. Her thin white arms are bare; she is wearing six or eight very thin wire bracelets that you will hear tinkling when we get closer to her. Right now the woman is curling her body against Dean's side and folding her arm under his, and she is rubbing her cheek on his shoulder like a cat rubbing its side against its master's leg. The gesture is expressive: she clings, pulls herself into the warmth of his body as if the caress could absorb some kind of consolation, as if Dean's side and the warmth of his body were the analgesic for some kind of pain inside her. Except that in her case the gesture is not much more than a manner, a habit—mere leaning against another body.

Now take a close look at the woman's face, now that she is turning to look up at Dean. Her eyes are large, and they look all the larger because they are so heavily made up. Now she is gazing at Dean's face, and her eyes widen like those of a silent movie heroine getting damp and filling with some effulgent feeling that I myself can't name. She looks down again, and rolls her forehead against Dean's shoulder, like a woman trying to get a hold of herself after the onset of grief or pity or remorse. When she looks up again—now—and we see the eyes once more, they are entirely inexpressive. She looks up at Dean, but Dean is calmly looking out into the street.

Dean sees David: "Hey, Dave buddy, over here!"

Then David hears Dean's voice; he knows where it is coming from and, without looking in that direction, pictures his companion waiting by the limousine. David doesn't look because he doesn't want to—looking would ruin everything, and everything would hurt too much. But just the same everything is over—all the feelings of lightness and the buoyancy of his heart just a few moments ago. At the sound of Dean's voice, David's little boy's feelings dissipated, jumped like frightened fish and then were gone. Imagine David walking out in the street there: imagine that there are beams of light radiating in every direction from his moving form, that they form some kind of halo on the pavement. When Dean speaks, it is as though the light forming the halo were extinguished at its source, so that it disappears. It is still there in a sense, but its circle, its orb, has to be supplied by the imagination. Unseen, it is everywhere.

"Hey, buddy! Over here!"

By now David can see Dean and the woman. Their bodies

are made visible by the same tiny film of light that is making the bars of the gate stark at the mouth of the arcade.

David turns to them and his stiff walk grows more awkward, more uncertain. When he is close enough for them to see his lips move, hear his very soft voice, he nods and he says an almost inaudible "Hi." The woman relaxes her crouch against Dean's side and stands erect, as if trying to be polite, waiting to be introduced. Her hands hang loose; she slips her arm out from Dean's. The woman's eyes are heavily made up; she is wearing a little pale orange lipstick and a very light powder. While she waits for somebody to say something her lips are a little anxious. They are turning in a strange way, and her eyes still seem full, and she keeps glancing at Dean.

"Hi, buddy."

After Dean's greeting, no one in the group of three seems able to speak. Dean's face is still; he obviously hasn't managed to introduce the woman leaning at his side. There is one chance in a million that David has anything to say. Meanwhile the woman continues to glance at Dean. Her lower lip curls inward. She relaxes. Her eyes are unstill. She extends her hand.

"My name is Barbara. Barbara Raeford."

David shakes her hand and gives his own name in a voice that is still scarcely audible. But Barbara Raeford doesn't need to hear David's name, since Dean has already told it to her.

But she realizes that she is expected to say something.

"I understand this car belongs to you."

"Yes."

"It's *very* beautiful."

David does not reply.

"Buddy. Uh. Barbara here needs a ride back to her place. So waddaya say we take her back; it'll take us a little while, because she lives over in New Jersey, but it shouldn't be too bad because her place is just over the bridge. So is it O.K.?"

David answers immediately, but without feeling anything. "Yes. That's all right. I don't mind."

"Oh, thank you *very* much. It's really such a help to me. I'm really very grateful."

Neither David nor Dean replies. They walk to the car.

Barbara Raeford lives in a five-hundred-foot tower of glass and reinforced concrete on the New Jersey bank of the Hudson, and you get to her house by making figure eights through cloverleaf after cloverleaf of superhighway after superhighway —all while tens of thousands of headlights are effortlessly gliding at seventy miles per hour all around you, making big arcs and circles and streaking long double lines. Barbara Raeford's apartment is on the thirty-second floor of her building. She is the recently promoted advertising manager of a women's shoe manufacturing concern. She lives all alone.

Right now Barbara Raeford is sitting between David and Dean, sitting stiffly, as if she were mad at somebody, and she is noticing from the feel along her buttocks and back how very much more luxurious soft leather is than felt. She is looking at the walnut dashboard and the big black car has begun to move. It has just turned past the Bayard Building, but only David glances out the window to see the swirling, lit concrete. Now they are moving through the Village on their way to the West Side and the entrance to the West Side Highway. The lights are changing from the lights of slums to the lights of the Village and its carnival, to the wealthy streets where there are houses with polished front doors, and then into the blackness of more warehouse ground. Dean is driving silently and

106

expertly, and David sits to Barbara Raeford's right so inconspicuously he seems almost absent. Dean expands his big chest with a rough, deep sigh, and that makes his belt creak at his waist. His sigh and the conventionally sexy sound make Barbara Raeford stop being so stiff. She melts again. Her head touches Dean's big shoulder.

On the highway, the car eases past huge riveted steel abutments and then begins to sail by piers and ships, past high gabled structures on the docks and past cranes and hanging cables. They pass words, all white or black or red in their spotlights—MICHELANGELO: UNITED STATES: FRANCE: CUNARD: UNITED FRUIT: ISBRANDTSEN: SPRY: QUEEN ELIZABETH: LEONARDO DA VINCI: SWEDISH AMERICAN LINES: AMERICAN PIONEER LINES: AMERICA: ALITALIA—while millions of light bulbs flutter in the deep space of the Manhattan skyline, and the car passes a bottle of Pepsi-Cola the size of a blimp pouring rivers of rippling blue neon tubes. There are cars all around them, everywhere, and everywhere there is the unchanging sound of the singing pavement under thousands of tires. In a minute they will be able to see the George Washington Bridge, a filament of blue over the black, streaked water, but now the car is passing a high, yellowish-brown ship, and they can see its name in black letters on the lofty white gunwale.

And then they cross that bridge.

On the drive to Barbara Raeford's apartment building in New Jersey, two events are going to take place. The first will be an argument between Dean and Barbara about some subject that is not clear. The second will be an accident on the highway to which all three of them will be witnesses.

Without moving away from Dean's side to sit up straight,

Barbara says to Dean in a whining voice, "Dean honey? Dean? You know, sweetie, I think it was a big mistake for you to come in tonight. It really was."

Barbara clings more tightly to his arm, so that the denim around his biceps twists.

"It really was a big mistake, sweetie? By now you ought to know that he doesn't like that: it only makes things worse for everybody. You really . . ."

Dean feels as though this attack from the woman beside him were unexpected. It seems to him that he had planned to spend the whole evening hearing only good words from her. He is self-deceived. He has been expecting the diatribe, just as he has been expecting the recoil which is invading his sensibility right now. Dean wishes that Barbara Raeford were dead. He would like to be stamping on her body. He wishes he were driving a corpse to New Jersey and wishes his destination were the deserted, black industrial swamps. Now that she has spoken, he knows that he is expected to answer her and begin to participate in the ritual she has inaugurated, but he refuses to. Everything in him refuses to. This refusal is part of the ritual.

Rather than reply, Dean imagines something.

Dean imagines this: David and Dean and Barbara Raeford have driven up in the limousine outside a big discotheque in a secluded part of New York, and all across its great big front there are changing, programmed lights glittering its name: THE ELECTRIC CIRCUS. THE ELECTRIC CIRCUS. THE ELECTRIC CIRCUS. The façade of the Electric Circus smears dripping red lights across itself and everyone around it, while the cataclysmic noise shakes from the windows and doors, like a siren wailing inside an operating room, making the padded swinging doors tremble. Girls in vinyl short skirts laugh, and their hair hangs to their waists. One of them turns to the arriving party and spreads her legs in a manly pose and displays behind the transparent plastic of her dress the swaying, curving turn of her groin, which sways with her unsteady posture. Her pubic hair is light brown. Suddenly the girl sinks to her knees, which draw up tight against each other, and she curls in a womb posture of despair. As the three of them pass, they see her untouched face against the painted cement. The girl is sobbing.

At the door, a young man in light-blue pants crouches beside a Negro who lies across the steps that lead into the dancing hall. The Negro is on the verge of passing out, and he is struggling to keep his friend's face clear in his eyes. The white boy leans over him, and his blond hair hangs over his cheeks. He holds his friend's dark face in his hands, and he is saying something that cannot be heard.

Now the arrival at this imaginary discotheque begins again in Dean's mind; he wants to see it all again.

Again, the limousine pulls up outside the dance hall, and its black polish begins to reflect the red and green and blue and orange lights that play over everything: the people, the cars, the concrete, the scrawny trees planted in the sidewalks, lights that play over their own faces as they sit in the back seat, driven by a chauffeur. Barbara Raeford's limp head lolls on Dean's shoulder, and David is sitting inconspicuous somewhere—Dean hardly notices him on the seat. David's doing something: looking at the back of the chauffeur's head maybe.

Then there is all the noise: the music, the rock and roll, the pounding floor of the dance hall, the girls screaming, the boy's moans.

The arrival at the discotheque starts all over again in Dean's mind. He feels the car pulling up in front of the building and then the door swings open so he can hear the trembling decibels of music and human sound filling the street, hear the voices laughing, shouting, calling each other's names like animals squealing in boxcars.

When the limousine door opens Barbara Raeford's face is transfigured with pleasure and she lets the sound and the lurid lights roll over her for a moment, her smile and her eyes seeming to lap at them, as if they had some kind of taste. Before she gets out of the car she turns to Dean and plants a soft orange kiss on his cheek. Both of them have stepped onto the throbbing sidewalk before David has turned to look out of the car and see where they are, but now David turns, too, and slides across the leather seat to get out. The facade of the Electric Circus smears dripping red light across itself and everything around it—the building is like a squealing baby smearing itself with its pablum. Clustered at four or five points on the sidewalk are little strands of girls wearing long hair and very short skirts, and now one of them sways like a balloon in the Macy's parade and with a trilling surge of music floats toward them, her hands planted on her hips and her legs apart so that one can see through the transparent plastic of her skirt her curving groin and the little flossy triangle of brown pubic hair, moving back and forth, in and out.

"Oh my *God*, Dean, look at that!"

The girl's groin undulates and her face can't be seen. (David is standing behind Dean and Barbara.) The girl keeps her hands on her hips and shrieks a long, long laugh that almost rides above the sound of the music, and now she flings one of the long tresses of her hair back over her shoulder and then in a single convulsive twitch she grips one of her breasts and her face becomes twisted and her mouth pulls into a grimace that looks as if blood may drool out of it. The girl begins to kneel. Her knees scrape together on the concrete, and as they do she curls laterally toward the sidewalk and assumes the womb posture. Barbara Raeford again takes Dean's arm and they step over the child's body, toward the steps that lead to the discotheque entrance.

Now this movement begins again in Dean's mind. As the girl sinks out of their field of vision, he is conscious of Barbara Raeford's intense, unreadable gaze against him. She has lifted her hand and touched his cheek. He turns to her, and he sees her laughing orange lips, and then the two of them step past the prostrate girl and move toward the painted steps—black, red, green, yellow, white—that lead to the discotheque's entrance below. In the stairwell, in front of the door, they see a Negro in red trousers lying across the three steps that lead upward again into the hall. He is almost unconscious, and struggles to keep looking at the face of a young man who crouches over him, slowly and carefully repeating something that cannot be heard. Even though the Negro's large, soft body lies across the steps, there is still a narrow path clear, so that Dean and Barbara can go in without stepping over him. She still holds his arm, but before they go in Dean turns back to look for the young man behind them, whom he now remembers. He sees David; he is kneeling beside the girl in the transparent dress. He has brought his face very close to hers. He is seeing nothing else. He seems far away, set apart by a screen of gibbering voices unconnected with bodies, voices squealing and giggling, shouting names. All those bodies are moving, moving around the two people bent on the sidewalk, moving unaware of what they see. They jump (Dean sees the girl's flashing legs); they wave their arms; they sway in their bright clothes; bodies embrace other bodies, which then turn away and are reassumed into the modulating static of human sound that flickers in the assaulted night air. Dean sees the girls' long dark hair everywhere. Everywhere he sees boys' wide smiles and their hips. David still crouches on the sidewalk. Dean sees that he has drawn the girl's hair out of her eyes. He can see the boy's lips moving; he is saying something that cannot be heard, saying it so close to her face that his breath moves on her face, moves on her skin. The girl can feel David's breath touching her eyes.

>-

Dean has made the car swerve again, and Barbara repeats herself.

"But just the same, you really shouldn't have come in tonight, Dean, you really shouldn't have. You know he doesn't like it."

Dean replies reluctantly. The car is under calm control.

"Why not, baby? He gave me a key, didn't he? So I came in. What's wrong with that, if the son-of-a-bitch gave me a key?"

"Of course you do, Dean sweetie, of course you have a key. But just the same you shouldn't have come except at the regular time."

"Well, I don't see why I shouldn't if he gave me a key and the run of the place."

"Well, of course you have a key, honey." (Barbara snaps this sentence in exasperation as she huddles more closely at Dean's side.) "What difference does that make, sweetie? Really—what difference does that make in the whole world?"

"Makes all the difference. The key is mine, and I show up when I feel like it."

Now the car is on the straightaway of a New Jersey highway. It is moving very fast.

"It makes all the difference."

"Let me decide that, Barbara."

"Let you decide what, sweetie?"

"Let me decide what makes a difference."

"But really, sweetie, it does make all the difference, that's what you don't seem to understand."

"And stop leaning against me, O.K., Barby?"

Barbara Raeford immediately sits straight in the seat and crosses her hands in her lap. She turns, looks into David's face and sees that her host has been watching her while all this has been going on, and that even under her angry gaze he doesn't turn away. And so she turns away instead, and her eyes fill up again with her silent-movie-star emotion. Barbara Raeford doesn't look as if she is angry. Her skirt lies flat on her legs, and her knees are bare. She rubs her hand on her knee.

David has been steadily watching both Dean and Barbara, and at the same time he has been trying not to see or understand. But now he begins to imagine Dean and Barbara together. He begins to see them in his mind's eye, picture them as lovers.

David sees this: David sees Dean, sees Dean's head bent a little to one side with his dark eyes half closed. They are not closed in a sexy way. They are closed in a kind of anger. Dean is thinking something over, he is about to make a decision, and when he has made it you will see it show on his face, on his forehead, in his eyes, in the twist of his jaw—and when you

113

can see that change Dean will be feeling better, meaner. Dean is thinking about Barbara, getting ready to meet her and deal with her anger, her hatred of him. The decision about how to deal with the anger is beginning to show on Dean's face now, though it isn't really clear yet, really formed. In a minute it will be, and Dean's features will compose into disdain.

David sees this: David sees Barbara Raeford. She is indoors somewhere, and she is waiting for Dean to show up for a visit. She is impatient and angry, looking like a woman who is holding on tight until some damn bore gets done talking so that she can snap back her angry reply. Barbara already knows what the guy is saying, and she despises it as much as she despises him. She tolerates him only out of the most strained kind of politeness, tense with her wish to rebut him, to attack —and she listens to him only so she can figure out the meanest way to come back with her angry reply.

That anger is steady and cold, cold enough to let Barbara wait a long time before she strikes. By this time she isn't even listening to him any more. All this is obvious, written all over her face, and in a minute when the real Dean really comes to knock at her door all Barbara Raeford's frigid anger will compose into a trembly, pouting *moue.*

This is what David Fontana sees: He sees a naked man and a naked woman in a room with stains on its walls. He sees their hatred; he sees the woman's slow caress across the man's cheek; he sees the man smiling under it. He sees the man gathering the woman into his arms and he sees their lips, male and female, curling against each other, and cold.

David closes his eyes and sinks back into the seat while he feels his rigid feelings without begin to soften and collapse into each other, falling like warm water through his body, and now his eyes close more tightly to shut out everything like light, everything like distance circulating around him like the spangled dome of a planetarium. In this tight darkness David's feelings start to pour upward, indistinguishable from one another, pity and fear and anger and isolation, all of them only words which he would never think of naming, all while something warm coalesces and surges behind his eyes.

And now David can see a woman's body. He sees her breasts, trembling, white, shaking, moving with her moving arms, the nipples curling toward him, peaking up and asking to be kissed and sucked; he sees the breasts and their tiny network of blue veins, the flesh washed with perfumed soap, caressed and softened in an oddly shaped bathtub, the red nipples coming through the soap and the girl curling her tongue across her lips for the camera; he sees her body stepping out of the tub, shaking and pure and dripping naked, breathing through its nostrils pure air, air pure to the point of filthiness. The face isn't seen any more. The flesh shakes and hangs. It is there only to be touched, only to be touched by a million hands.

And now there is a man's body, starting with a hand, moving to an arm that is rippling, the biceps bulges, ripples, grows hard, goes soft; the arm curves into the crevasses of tender-skin of the huge chest, skin so tender that a fingernail could scratch it or press it into a tiny, tickling fold. The chest is touched with curling reddish hair and it breathes, big, heavy, lusting, the skin delicate and white beneath the color. The spread thighs are huge, rippling and hard, soft again, hard under their down of man hair, and the huge penis is hanging, growing, a big vein across it bulging and the reddish, teeny slit at the tip of it untouchably tender, a lusting mouth. His testicles are big, in brownish skin, hanging, their flesh curling with rough reddish hair.

David squeezes his eyes closed and tries to call back the unnamed emotions; he is trying to feel something warm again instead of these pornographic tableaux, these jiggling film clips, these pin-point precise detail plates arranged for close inspection on the sides and in the corners of a landscape of anger. But David's feelings don't come back, they have drowned, they have sunk into his body and he can't reach them now, and the muscular pressure against his eyes is only intensifying the images' willful presence, only making their glossy, lusciously untouchable trashy precision blend and become redolent with the smell of slick paper, the feel of pages stuck together with sperm, with the feel of universal flesh, shaking, bulging, trembling, stiffening, touched and untouched, felt and unfelt, caressed by an absent hand, sopped into the seeing eyes, lapped up by lipless mouths, drooling, slapped to a pain that is not felt, kissed with the spit that flies into the paper faces and soothed with a love that dies on the skin like a last stinking, dying breath.

Right now that flesh is David's life, his extreme insight into the pattern that is carrying him into himself and along this highway at seventy miles an hour, the spectacle of which he is the sole spectator, one created solely for him, enacted before him despite his presence, arrested and frozen now in the single tremor on the untorn skin of two human bodies.

➤

Dean's anger is mounting against the woman at his side.

"You want to know something, Barby baby?—I don't know how many people I saw there, I saw lots of them, sweet-

116

heart, and I'll tell you something else, I saw *him*, and I think you ought to know, baby, that you are the first person to say a word, one damned little word against me coming in tonight. . . ."

Barbara Raeford is silent. Both her hands touch her knees. She says, very quietly, under her breath: "You saw who? I don't believe you. I just don't believe you."

"Listen, I didn't hear what you said, Barby baby. You were talking too quiet. I'll tell you something else, Barby, it doesn't matter *what* you said, Barby; it doesn't matter at all." Dean jams down the accelerator still farther, and the car begins to move, very gently, a little faster.

Barbara Raeford's feelings modulate. She curls, and spreads a sudden pout. She leans at his side.

"Oh, Dean honey, let's not fight about it."

"I said don't lean on me. I'm driving."

"Be a little nice to me."

"Be quiet."

"Be a little nice to me." Barbara Raeford leans against Dean. He does not seem to notice. He does not look at her.

David has settled down a little and grown calmer; he sits looking out into the spotty white lights that line the highway and recede into the flat New Jersey landscape. But inside David's mind all these patches of light don't cohere into a world. He might as well be drifting through the blackness of outer space, looking at circling white stars that no longer twinkle, or be floating through the snowstorm inside a television tube after broadcasting hours are over. Everything breaks apart; David's mind is numb; his eyes are staring, stupid and open-mouthed, as it were. He is sitting in the seat with his right leg slightly raised (the motorcycle helmet has been thrown into the back, where it nestles in a corner of the black leather rear seat), and he is resting his chin on his fist. He is not thinking.

Barbara Raeford is sitting straight again, and now she turns to have another look at the rich boy sitting beside her. This time she discovers that David is not looking at her, and that he is obviously not thinking about her. That makes her want to start talking.

"Are you an old friend of Dean's? David?"

David's fist drops into his lap. He turns to her rather slowly; his face does not express the distaste and annoyance he feels, and it could not express them. It seems bland, a little surprised to have been spoken to.

"Excuse me?"

"I guess you and Dean must be old buddies from way back?"

Dean does not move. He tilts his head to the side mirror again—à la Le Mans—and, when he's sure Barbara can't see his face, he smirks to himself.

"No," David says. "I mean yes. Yes. We *do* know each other."

Barbara Raeford smiles again. She has decided that David is a child with whom she must make an effort to be patient, so that when she speaks again her voice stops just short of a babyish coo.

"Oh? But have you and Dean known each other for a long time?"

"Oh. No. We haven't."

The car is silent again.

"Oh. It's just that I can't understand where you met."

David has the impression that he speaks without deciding to do so.

"Dean works for my aunt."

"You mean Dorothy Fontana?"

David decides to ask Barbara how she knew his aunt's name.

"Oh, well. Dean told me her name a long time ago. Dean, don't you think that David is such a sweet boy?"

David looks toward Dean, who continues to tilt his head lazily, with his hand resting on the top of the wheel.

Neither of them speaks. Dean has not returned David's glance.

It was at this point in the drive that the accident occurred.

At that moment, approximately three hundred yards in front of the limousine there was visible crossing the highway an overpass with wooden railings, part of a road which led from an insignificant New Jersey town—merely a collection of early-twentieth-century houses filthy with the dirt of impoverished industrial suburban slums—into a highway which had at no time been significant, but which had fallen into a desuetude, transformed into a service road, after the superhighway was opened. This overpass carries very little traffic; late at night it is almost deserted. At that moment, for reasons the police were never able to discover, a girl seventeen years old was walking down the center of the overpass road, alone. She had been drinking; she was slowly drawing one bare foot in front of another, pacing out the center line, muttering to herself, swinging a pair of high-heeled shoes in her hand. Shortly before she reached the center of the bridge's span, she imagined that she heard the roar of a racing automobile bearing down on her from behind—the wild sound of the engine screaming and racing behind her seemed insanely close—and she spun around, her shoes sailing from her hand in opposite directions. She was drunk, she was terrified. The confused child imagined in a flash that she was confronting the violent glare of the headlights, close enough to smash into her body and strike her down before she even had the chance to spin away from them again. She screamed, screamed a sound that was only a sound, wholly unrecognizable and wholly unlike the stage screams one is accustomed to hearing in the mass media, a sound that choked on itself as it grew, and then the girl turned wildly and began to run, and in an instant she was hurtling very fast with the weight of her body flung forward so that she wasn't carrying her own weight, but was rather carried by it, headlong, almost as if she were chasing herself. She was blind; she saw nothing as she rushed toward the guardrails: she did not see the car which she imagined was about to kill her; she did not see the highway below; she did not see the night; she did not see the wooden railings of the overpass. It seemed that her legs were flying behind her; they could not keep up with the thrust of her own violent thrust forward, and that self-extinguishing sound kept growling in her throat, choking her on a rush of air she could not feel and screaming around her deaf ears; she could not distinguish between inhaling and exhaling, between screaming and gasping for breath. She did not feel her bare feet spraying pebbles behind her. Her arms spread and her body slammed into the railing as a fumbling diver slaps flat into the water, her head flung back, her torso smacking across the unyielding substance which now yielded; the gravelly planks swung from their posts with a wooden squeal, rusty nails ripped from their holes or broke and the girl swung out over the wood like somebody rolling across a seesaw. Her arms flailed, and her last thought was to grasp the plank against her body, which had broken loose from its support; but she held nothing; the wood scraped her arm and ripped her dress and then was gone; there was nothing near her and she fell free (just as David and Dean, three hundred yards away, saw the movement on the overpass), fell soundlessly.

Immediately, David and Dean know what they have seen. Dean's foot flicks from the accelerator and immediately begins to tap the power brake gently, while David stiffens and lurches forward in the seat, slapping his hand against the walnut dashboard in his strange rhythm of cognition. But Barbara Raeford has seen the girl fall without comprehending it. Only after the scene on the overpass is still, the plank dangling from its bridge, does she grasp what has happened, and then she releases a scream—a familiar, theatrical one this time—and she pulls back wildly in her seat with a frightened muscular reflex of someone beside the driver pushing on the floor where the brake might be and she is pulling at her hair.

"Dean! Dean! Somebody *fell* out there. Somebody fell! *Somebody fell!*"

Dean answers her and their voices become mixed in a rattle of exclamations that bat through the car like a rubber ball ricocheting from wall to wall. Even David says something, but he is not heard. Dean's voice is calm until Barbara Raeford silences him by violently imploring him.

"Dean, it's terrible, Dean, don't stop, Dean, don't stop, please don't stop, please don't stop, Dean, please please please don't stop. . . ."

Barbara is flailing back and forth on the seat while Dean swings his head around to check the traffic behind him, and suddenly David knows that Dean is afraid, terribly afraid, that his movements in the driver's seat are the reflexes of a man running for his life. David's body is suddenly sucked into the seat as Dean slams down the accelerator and the car jumps. Dean is pulling forward in the seat, hunching on the wheel, and David feels everything inside him stopping when he sees that Dean's face is like wax.

"Please don't stop, Dean, please please please don't stop, please . . ."

Dean has panicked and the car is speeding, tracking a lateral across the highway, moving into the lane farthest from the one where the girl lies. Dean's eyes are bright; they flick in their sockets; he moves with the flawless grace of a fleeing animal. Terror has put Dean in complete command of his job, and his hands move like instruments of flesh. His leather gloves aren't an affectation any more; they have fused with the steering wheel they touch. The escape from the accident is executed by a perfect body, a body like that of an animal crouching just before its hindquarters kick and it bolts. The long black car gains speed, and David, still pushing his hands against the dashboard, straining to see while he strains to look away, gets one short glimpse of the girl's smashed body and he sees all the cars stopping, sees the open doors and the drivers, mostly men, running—one of them running very fast, away from the spot, toward a ditch.

But now the limousine has passed under the bridge and come out on the other side, where the oncoming traffic across the center island is approaching at a steady speed, entirely unaware.

Now David feels his own fear begin to race through his body, imagining he can see the dead girl's face, a dead face though perhaps her body is somehow still alive, still bleeding and breathing. David sees her face looking up at him, and her eyes stare, and the blood is coagulating on her ripped cheek and smashed forehead. David's fear is intense now, wild in his ears as he bends forward and tries to hold on even though it feels to him that the car has careered out of control, that there is going to be another accident, that they are going to crash, and immediately David remembers that he can make it happen, that he is still Dean's employer, that he has the power to command. His lips start to move and he turns to Dean again, but all he sees is Barbara Raeford leaning against Dean, her hands covering her face. . . .

David turns away and looks forward, leans forward, aching to shout at Dean and make him stop the car—stop it, stop it, you've got to stop, you *can't*—but even though the shouting is just about to jump out of his throat the way tears come into some people's eyes, nothing, not one sound comes out of David and he remains still, turning spastically in his seat, glancing around with pained, tortured eyes, from the open highway ahead of them, over to Dean's hard, self-absorbed, imperious face, and back to the rear window, the cluster of stopped cars and running drivers that has now almost dropped out of sight. David's eyes flutter like imprisoned animals trying to find some opening to run through and escape, but he doesn't find any opening, and the gasping emotions that his terror has raised stay silent.

By now Dean has grown calm enough to be aware of the other people in the car, and the first person he senses there is not Barbara but David, who is leaning forward with his

123

tense eyes that seem to be almost bursting as they stare. Dean feels safer now and his muscles have started to relax. He lets the speedometer gently dip from around eighty to sixty-five, while his hands, which were clutched almost side by side at the top of the wheel, slide back to their right positions at two and ten, and he leans back into the seat a bit. Dean takes a couple of looks out the rear-view mirror. The muscles in his thighs are getting softer.

Stiff and fearful though he is, David picks up this change in feeling from Dean and he has begun to grow calmer, too. The animal sense of danger—the bristling back, the surge of all that adrenaline and acid, the muscles straining and taut—is ebbing now and being replaced by a wave of creaturely complacency flowing from Dean's body past Barbara Raeford and over him like something warm, like air. Dean keeps his eyes on the road; his gestures are only for his driving and remain strictly functional. Dean doesn't turn to either of his companions: his body is still absorbed in a single task, while David lets his own body relax into the seat and the muscles in his arm, like Dean's, grow looser, touched with the aftertaste of their tension. David's abdomen relaxes into softness and now moves slowly, following the rhythm of his breathing chest. He draws a deep breath and exhales so audibly that the others probably hear. The backs of David's legs are soft on the warm black leather of the seat. Barbara Raeford is quietly curled beside Dean, docile as a baby sucking its thumb, and David is no longer conscious of her. He is only half-aware. Barbara is like someone who has not yet been quite forgotten, who is still in the back of his mind.

Just for a second, Dean thinks of saying something to relieve the silence that has settled down in the car, but when the impulse to speak doesn't find any words, he shunts the whole idea out of his mind and dumps it. Dean isn't like David; he can't just reach for and get some meaningless phrase, some list of sounds that will let him say something when he feels the requirement to speak leveled against him like the waiting expression on a face. So in one snappy twist of thought the inarticulate impulse to speak—say something, let them hear you say something—is disobeyed and forgotten. Dean's legs move a little on the seat. He wets his lips. He drives. True enough, something like thoughts are moving around in his mind, but they aren't real yet. To say something, Dean needs someone to say it to. He needs someplace to say it. He needs everyone's watching eyes. Just the same, the accident and his role as driver are converging now in his mind, moving into and across one another, even though everything in his consciousness remains unspoken, unarticulated, even to himself. What is he feeling? He is feeling what is about to be guilt, unnamed, and what is about to be pride. There is anger. There is a little pity. All of them rising and then sinking away out of awareness like the slow rhythms of a kaleidoscope; muted colors not yet fully visible, turning and falling away and forming themselves again behind a colorless veil that drains them of their color, all of them unstable crystals of every shade, all of them, every feeling appearing and disappearing at once.

Meanwhile, David's pity is subsiding into passivity, although his inertia hasn't gotten hard around him yet, hasn't stunned him again like the sudden thudding thrust of somebody's hand shoving him back, with a jerk, into obscurity. Even though David is looking straight ahead, he is conscious only of Dean's presence in the car. He is looking ahead, seeing, but unaware of, the passing road signs, the black-and-white pavement, the blowing grass and the factories with their smoke and light beyond. He is losing himself again, like a child who has stepped through a glimmering mirror, as if he were hypnotized, never looking back, stepping into the shapeless light of his absent feelings, all of which nonetheless remain somewhere in him, working and turning. He has the impression of wondering about something, and yet he wonders about things that are still abstract in his mind, and he questions them wordlessly, feeling only the tiny stabbing impression of the questioning without its substance. He has let Barbara Raeford fade away into nonexistence, and still, there she is, curled and pouting, mocking fear; blond in her orange make-up; her cream-colored dress riding up on her thighs, so they become more and more visible, flashing on the leather seat; her knees bare and shivering just a little now and then, her breasts hanging loose under the loose cloth, the nipples outlined and clear. There is Dean, his thighs resting on the seat, his dungarees tight across his curving, bulging crotch, his torso heavy and breathing in the denim shirt. There is his black hair. His eyes. His private smile. All of this is lost on David, as the world is lost on someone breathing under anesthesia, as touch is lost on the addict of light, or as sound is lost on the *débauché* of skin. And yet somewhere in his feelings, which are scattered like flickering shattered lines jerking arhythmically across the eye of an oscilloscope, David is still conscious of physicality. Conscious of it still working through nerves that seem to lead through feelingless flesh, out of his dying body into nowhere. Conscious of nothing else.

➤

Harriet is relaxing in the chair by the window of the turret room. She is thinking about their troubled, flawless bond, about her brother hiding up here in the red sandstone turret or of herself hiding with him in the dressing room of the unused bedroom, with its draperies all splashy flowers, with the satin couch where David stood, in black pants, coding his secret ballet with waves and jerks. In her mind's eye, she sees him standing there and a little slosh of pity falls inside her and she smiles. Her back is to the door, but if you look in you will see her bend her head, and see her brownish hair shake a little as the tiny wave of that womanly emotion comes, and then is gone.

Harriet feels like an invader here. The turret room is so dark that it seems to her like a box with no inside, and she is aware only of the window opening onto the empty space beyond. Her own body turns a little in the chair, and she feels in her sleepy reflections that the chair and her body are the only things in the room; that there is not even air, not even darkness. Stand back a little and you'll get a different angle on things. Now you can see her bare feet. She has pushed off her slippers (they are under the chair). She rests her head on her fist, and now she bends her toes, pushing against the baseboard in front of her. There is a small sound. She sighs.

Her sigh has made her see something. *This is what she sees.*

Harriet imagines that she is with her lover on a yacht on the open sea. The clouds are so high in the brilliant whiteness above her that it seems incredible that they are visible at all, and yet you can see them, even see them moving up there in what must almost be the stratosphere. She disregards the walnut deck chairs and the little riveted white tables set permanently in a casual angle to them, and lies instead on a brown straw mat spread out on the deck, her eyes darkened, protected from the glaring blue green by sunglasses. She closes her eyes. She peeks out sometimes at all that color and then she closes her eyes again and gives in to the warm rubbing of the sun against her abdomen, and she likes the tiny roughness of the deck planks against the base of her spine. She is covered with oil and the clean sea is littered with boats nearby, but they could as well be a thousand miles away, drifting near an equator she has never seen. The northern sun has turned tropical. Harriet tastes the wet oil on her lips.

Harriet puts David in a hiding place in the cabin; but she does not know he is there. The cabin is small, though large for that of a yacht, and is punctuated with affected portholes and expensive lamps in gold shades, designed to make it look like home. Sitting there in the chair of the turret room and lying there on the deck, she casts around in her mind for someplace in the cabin to hide her brother, but she can't find one. David is hidden in her just the same, unknown to herself and to her lover. Let him just be there unknown. Let him be invisible.

Harriet's lover is standing on a higher deck. He is moving, bending, pulling, and his shirt is off; no—maybe he is still wearing it, a thin blue knit shirt, tight across his chest, a little bit wet with sweat, although the sweat immediately evaporates in the hot sun and then there is more. His hair is black in the brilliant light. His thighs are tight, brown and sunburned; they relax, then they are tight again. The hair on his legs is black. Harriet is looking away, out to sea. She sees him on the deck at the same time. His back is turned. She doesn't see his face.

In the turret room, Harriet shifts in her chair and her hand drops. There, you can see it dangling on the arm of the chair;

her fingers flick and jump, and now she pulls it out of our line of vision, onto her lap. She pushes with her toes against the baseboard again. She is nervous. Now she is still. Her hand returns, and rests on the chair's arm, moving a little, in an imperceptibly jumpy way. Now it is still.

Harriet sees the yacht again. *This is what she sees*: She sees it drifting in the green sea and she hears the water splashing and rolling at the gunwales; she imagines she can feel the thin spume of water the boat throws up as it moves, even though the deck is dry. The sea is flowing loose and broad and empty in all the wet flatness that rolls away in every direction, and at the same time it seems like a web that flutters around the paperweight of the rocking boat at its center. Again, Harriet imagines that she is sprinkled with the green spray even though the deck is dry and the varnish is rough and hot in the scratching, numbing glare.

He is beside her and her eyes are closed. His hand kneads the brown, soft flesh of her abdomen, feels the tiny hairs on her skin, hairs almost invisible, down left a little sticky from the evaporated oil. His hand skitters across the inside of her thigh and squeezes it. His lips are somewhere on her face. Soft, tight, hard. And now Harriet hears the thudding of a fist on the deck, pounding like the padded sticks of a tympani, rumbling with a ferocious staccato anger that fills her ears so that she jerks around, and now she sees her brother's thin arms beating the wood while she sees his harsh, angry eyes opening and closing, seeing only her, beating almost with the same ferocity that drives his fists. She sees David's lips—trembling and tight and wet, open and sucking the air as if he were inhaling a soundless scream—as if she were falling through the empty sky. The warm, heavy body beside her is soft, some-

129

thing she has got to shove away, but it is only pulling closer, so close that it seems to be all flesh and at the same time all breath around her, almost covering her.

This is what Harriet sees: She sees a boy's body bent in pain over a man who is struggling beneath him. She sees a man's arm fending off the pounding anger of young beating fists. She sees someone's face turned away from hers. She sees his teeth clenched and she sees his eyes, wide with an unseeing stare of violated incomprehension. She sees someone's face turned downward, his body shaking and his arms flashing in an arpeggio of anger.

This is what Harriet hears: Now she doesn't hear anything except the stumbling, wandering ocean around her.

This is what she sees: She sees angry eyes and an adolescent's unmanageable tears. She sees someone's face turned away from her as he lies on the deck. She sees the fists still clenched, even though the arms are still.

This is what she hears: She hears somebody shouting at her, and getting through to her, too, though she can't make out the words. She hears a shouting moan undulating into language.

This is what she sees: She sees a face, all torn, coming closer. Now it is close enough for her to hear the sound of anger on the skin; close enough to touch.

➤

Harriet stands up, pushes back that chair, and leans against the sill, looking down onto the dark lawn. The darkness in the room is at her back, filling the room like an odorless opaque gas, and the little remaining moonlight spreads just enough light to outline her silhouette where she stands. She sees the unlit grass, the dark garage and its brown doors, lighter planes set in the edgeless complex of buildings below. She shifts her weight, and leans on her right arm. In a moment, she will sit down again.

She closes her eyes and leans; she wants to sleep. She sees the boat again, tries to feel the sun rubbing her skin. She leaves the window sill and sits again in the chair. She is quiet. She can't quite think, and yet her mind is gathered up into that knot of mental attention that feels like concentrated thought. She crosses her legs, and rubs her toes together as she slightly extends her foot, firm and straight, like a ballerina's. She looks up again at the window. She closes her eyes again. Look at her hand on the chair's arm. It's not moving, it's still.

⊁

In the bedroom below, Dorothy is asleep in the same negligee she wore all evening. Her dresser is a bulbing, rococo antique affair, enameled, sprinkled with pale blue and red flowers. Her chaise longue is covered with blue chintz; maybe the chintz is a little torn. Dorothy herself looks like a lump of cloth on the bed. There she sprawls, snoring away, conked out without the chance of a single dream.

⊁

Upstairs in the turret room, Harriet dozes in the chair, exhausted after all that waiting and muddled after this evening's sequence of her sharp, strong, framed emotions. Harriet isn't sleeping deeply yet, so that she is still a little bit in touch with her body, still a little bit aware of the odd discomfort of sleeping in a chair. Her sleeping face is bent downward, out of line with the window. By the time the limousine at last comes up the driveway to the garage (its headlights the only lights in

131

what will by then be total darkness), she will be sleeping so deeply that neither the light nor the sound will wake her, even though the sash is raised all the way. The car has not yet come. A little breeze is blowing on Harriet's hair.

➤

I can't tell you what time it is now, or where the car was when Harriet drifted off to sleep. Right now the car is moving somewhere on the Long Island Expressway. The trip back across Manhattan has been made. It has been almost an hour since Dean and David left Barbara Raeford in the glassy, creamy light of her apartment tower. Even though they are rather near Islip, David has not yet thought of getting home again, not yet anticipated the dark house on the hill, or the curving turn (taken slowly this time) through the gate.

➤

Look at the two of them, there in the front seat, behind the glass. Dean might be expected to be slumping with fatigue by this time, but he is still sitting straight in the seat, and his hands still rest on the wheel at two and ten. The leather gloves are dry and delicate on his fingers; his black hair is smooth, freshly combed (after Barbara Raeford disappeared into the glass lobby of her apartment tower, Dean took a look into the rear-view mirror, pulled a long comb from his back pocket, and ran it through his hair with five fast, complicated strokes of his hand) and the muscles on the back of his neck are full and tight; the soft cloth of his denim collar curls a little with their occasional small movements. Dean is quiet and conscious; waiting for something. He is still and alive.

You can get some idea of the late hour by taking a look at the traffic on the expressway. We've passed only eight or ten cars in the past two or three minutes. None of them travel at the ordinary speed; they travel either very slowly or very fast. Dean is traveling very fast.

David has turned so that he faces Dean, and his profile is made a mute chiaroscuro by the dash lights, and the thin, constant electric illumination outside. His face is still, and he watches with the same expressionless disengagement we have seen all evening. He watches as if he were not seen.

Up there behind the glass, this is going on:

Dean is tapping the heel of his left foot on the carpeted floor, and his thigh bounces in an uneven rhythm. The rest of his body does not move. Once in a while, he glances at David without turning his head. He relaxes, and stops the tapping movement. His right leg turns outward, so that without moving his foot from the accelerator, he spreads his legs.

He has begun to feel the close, dull presence of David's gaze, and the annoyance he felt from the beginning, a little bit, a little vaguely, is now there, on his mind, pestering him. David's expression remains unchanged. Dean has this quick fantasy: he imagines that he slaps David's face. Now he makes a move. He wants to talk.

"You don't still feel sick, do ya?"

David is slow to answer.

"No. I'm all right."

"I was wondering, because you still look pretty whacked out. It hit you hard. It must've really hit you hard."

David doesn't answer at all this time. His expression doesn't change, even though Dean has made this intrusion onto what had been tacitly forbidden since Dean stood by the window of the chalet looking toward the grove before he turned to David with his private smile, his leer: ("But you've been watching something, haven't you?").

Now, just as then, David refuses to answer, though his stomach grows tight and his back bristles.

Dean speaks again. "Didn't it? Huh?"

David answers with the same quiet voice. "Didn't it what?"

"Didn't it hit you hard?"

David is looking as fast as he can for some phrase, but he can't find one. He answers. "Didn't what?"

"Your sister? Huh?"

This is what David sees: He sees Harriet's face bent over Dean's. Dean's eyes are closed. Harriet is pressing the firm flesh of his cheeks with her fingers, and her eyes are full of love.

"Seeing your sister, huh?"

"My sister."

Dean says nothing.

"It really got to you, huh?"

David again does not answer for a moment. Then he does, very softly. "Yes. Yes, it did."

"Yeah. Because she's out there with that guy every other night, ya know. I mean, like, I won't say nasty words, but . . ."

The driver checks the rear-view mirror with a glance.

➤

Look at them up there in the front seat now. Dean is turning his head now and then, and he is talking slowly and steadily, and David's face remains still. The boy has not yet turned away. His expression has not changed. He listens now. He does not seem to be answering, or responding in any way at all.

This is what Dean is saying: "So I was different from you,

134

'cause I'd started playing around a long time before my sister knew anything at all about it, knew anything about anything, see. So, it didn't get to me so much when she started laying out for guys. See, I didn't think it was so bad, 'cause I'd been playing around myself. Doesn't get to you the same way when you've already played around like I'd been doing, hell, since I was twelve years old when I tried to stick my little dick up some little girl in a vacant lot. So that made things different."

Dean pulled back his shoulders and then rolled his back in the seat. He shifted his weight and flexed his right leg. He turned to the boy, and looked directly into his expressionless eyes. His own eyes were heavy and full. Now Dean knew that he was being heard. Now Dean knew that every word he said was working somewhere behind those eyes. He looked back to the road, and slowly rolled his right thigh in the seat.

"You've got to play around a lot. 'Cause you've got to find out about a lot. Before you ever get what you want."

David was still.

"I don't suppose you've done any of that yet, huh?"

David waits, as always, before he answers. "No."

➤

This is what happened when the car got back to the Fontana estate.

The lights on the driveway and the sound of the car did not wake Harriet, who was by then sleeping deeply in the chair. Her body was perfectly still, her head bent to one side. Her hands, which were a little damp, lay crossed on her lap, and the breeze, which was steady now, continually moved her hair, and her face seemed turned so as to avoid its touch. She slept there till dawn, when a strong morning wind woke her up.

Outside the closed garage, the car stops, and Dean, who

ended his monologue perhaps two or three minutes before they reached the gate, asks David if he will get out and press the key near the door frame that opens the electric door. But David doesn't answer. He doesn't move at all. His eyes do not look away, and he scarcely seems to notice that they have arrived. Dean remembers that he lacks the power even to make a simple request. Dean looks at him and once again stares at the expressionless eyes. Next he clips the key off the ring hanging from the dash, and lets himself out.

Dean turns the switch, and walks so he stands directly in front of the car, while the wide brown door rises. The lights blare against his dungarees and denim shirt. He cocks his head, and his secret smile returns. He seems to be looking in curiously through the windshield at the boy, who has turned to watch. As he stands in the headlights, Dean feels a small impulse to move his hips in a certain way, and like an actor quickly choosing and rejecting extemporaneous gestures, he decides against it. He walks back to the car and closes the door.

Next he slams the stick into reverse and spins out backward; when the car is forty feet from the door he drops the stick into drive and swings into an open space, and while the car is still turns the wheel again and again, eases the stick back into reverse and curves back into the driveway, going backward. During this maneuver, David doesn't move or even show surprise. The car eases backward into the garage at about two or three miles an hour. Dean stops, watches the door close in front of them. He turns off the ignition, pushes the plunger that douses the lights. Then he pulls the glove off his right hand, and lays his arm across the back of the seat, so that his fingers are a few inches from David's shoulder.

136

It's finally time to say something like "Well, we made it," or "O.K., we're here," or if nothing else just a curt little "O.K."—but something has got to officially put the cap on the long ride back and serve as the signal for both young men to climb out. David doesn't move, of course, doesn't speak, doesn't show a single sign that the ride is over, and a funny, fluttering twitch inside Dean suddenly makes him know that David's stillness shouldn't be interrupted—makes him know he isn't supposed to say, "O.K., we're here." Dean sits silent, his face immobile and vague in the darkness, not still with the fleshless visuality of David's unblinking stare, but quietly savoring the delicious wait, digesting the soft aggression of saying nothing at all. Rather than speaking, Dean shoots a quick glance and discovers David's dark eyes—touches of darkness in the hush that has settled across the front seat—as if they were two dead things. Dean realizes that David hasn't looked away even once since he got out to open the garage door, and that makes Dean jumpy in a way he likes, makes him a little shy and gives him a nice nasty little feeling. Rather than say anything, Dean looks away and his left hand gets nervous, so that he starts to fiddle with the plunger for the headlight, pushing and pulling it just a little—not enough to actually turn on the lights, but just jiggling it. With a jerk, Dean arches his torso, and he moves a little on the seat. There is the sound of his shifting weight and the clicking switch.

Outside, the sky is immense, black and moonless. Standing beside the garage door, you can hardly see the house, which is now entirely dark, every light out.

Dean pulls the plunger a little too hard and the green dash lights come on. Dean immediately snaps them off, as if they were hot, burning him.

But he keeps pulling at the control, and now the dash lights click on again, and they make the dark color of the front seat greenish. But rather than turning them off again, this time Dean clips another glance past David, wincing out of the corner of his eye as if David were too bright to look at.

He sees that David is still staring at him the way a sleepy dog stares at its master, and Dean flicks the lights off.

Dean looks away, out the front window, and he starts jiggling his hand on the light switch, back and forth, so that the tremulous, tough flesh of his fingers and forearm flutters, and he jerks out the plunger and all four headlights rise and ignite and turn the dull brown plane of the garage door into a blinding screen of light that fills the whole stall and makes the front seat seem daylit. Everything—the washed-out denim of Dean's shirt sleeve, the light-brown, expensive-looking fabric of David's trousers—everything is bright.

Dean again douses all the lights so that the darkness comes back. He makes a nervous laughing noise with his throat, and he makes use of the restored darkness to shift his eyes toward David again. Again, he sees David's unbroken, numb stare.

Dean pulls the dash lights back on, and this time leaves them going.

David can feel his heart pounding like some sound in a science-fiction movie—he can hear it booming like a depth charge in a submarine story. He knows that his face still looks as fake and dead as a plastic mask, and knows that his eyes seem blank, even though they seem to him just about to fill up with tears and start dribbling. David can't look away and he doesn't want to; his mind is swimming with his uncertainty about what Dean is going to do. David shifts his eyes a little so that now he's looking at Dean's big, jumpy hand on the light switch.

Dean pulls the dash lights back on and leaves them going this time. And now without looking at David he slowly lowers his right hand and reaches, touching, and now his hand lightly closes over David's wrist, but just at the instant his warm palm makes contact with David's arm Dean turns with an expression of steady, funny, tough, gentle decisiveness and starts pulling David's hand toward his crotch, pushing his fingers toward the big, still-soft basket, and after the first instant of resistance David's trembling arm gives and moves with Dean's strong, directing hand. Touching the bulging denim mound David feels the prick start to stir while Dean knows the erection will come on good and hard and his prick and his scrotum and his hair and the skin inside his thighs and the tenderness inside his butt start to turn on and tingle, and Dean starts to get the really tough need filling him up. Dean's mouth has come open, very slightly. He is looking directly into David's scared face.

Now David tries to jerk his hand away and Dean grabs it back again. And then again, and then they have their little tug of war until Dean starts to get mad about it and David is panicky and Dean is pushing his helpless fingers against the swelling groin and David is whining, "No! No! No! No! No!" whining as if he were about to cry and the no's sounding like sobs. But Dean's not taking any of that crap.

Now David starts fighting to get away, pulling and pushing against Dean's shoulder with his free hand, saying, *"No! No! I don't want to!"* But Dean's not taking any of that either, so he flips around in the seat and, swinging his free arm around David's shoulders, starts to squeeze inward with arms that are transformed into a soft, gentle, looplike vise that makes David's straining elbow crumble, and David falls inward toward Dean, he feels his scared face touching Dean's big face, smelling it, smelling the man smell on it and feeling his own boy's hands touching Dean's big, heavily breathing sides, feeling his own face sinking toward Dean's big, soft, breathing chest. But he now decides to stop hugging and with a heave he pulls David up and then flips him back, laying him out on the seat and pushing down after him, on top of him, while David jerks or flops like an animal without limbs. David submits like a friable piece of tubing, a straw, and now Dean's heavy, big, compact weight is on him, rolling on him, throbbing on him, and David can feel the huge erection hard against his thigh and he can look up to see Dean's big face right above him, or he can close his eyes and smell Dean's breath, even feel his chest moving when he says: "Like to play around, huh, kid? huh, rich kid? Like to fight, huh? huh?" coming down harder on David's body each time, bouncing on him, forcing him into the seat. Dean grabs his arm and lifting forces David's hand into his crotch again and David can feel the huge prick squished into the tight dungarees while Dean rolls his butt and pushes his full groin against David's hand and his terrified thigh.

Next Dean looks into David's closed, frightened face and snorts: "Sit up." He slides off David's body and sits straight himself. David pulls his hand free.

"Oh, no ya don't, buddy, oh, no ya don't," and he yanks the hand back. Dean's basket is huge and his arm is flaccid. David's fingers move over the bulging denim, wiggling, flicking.

Suddenly Dean shoves the gentle hand away. With one snap of his right hand he flips loose the buckle of his garrison belt and then, grunting a little grunt, pulls loose the snap of his jeans.

David watches the copper zipper of the fly spreading open, seeing the white of Dean's shorts come into the open like a spreading V of snow. There is some kind of body smell in the air, not ugly, but strong. David feels his arms tremble and his back is shaking, feeling as if it will crumble, and he wants to pull away because everything is shaking and making him feel like crying. But there won't be any crying here. David can tell that, from the outside, his eyes look wild. But, even though they are darting about in some crazy way, all David remembers seeing is the white V of Dean's shorts, and now his hairy, dark olive hands pulling the shorts down to let his big, surprising brown prick spring up and come free, sticking up like . . .

Dean's lips are wet. He turns and claps his hand around David's shaking neck and jerks the face down toward the upended prick, and next he feels David's tight, soft lips and tender cheeks fluttering on the horny sensitive tip. With one last, wild, spastic effort David tries to pull away again, and he manages to jerk his neck free and sit up again.

"No! No!" David is sure that he is going to cry, and somewhere within the peaceful core of his consciousness, some nodule of his being untouched even by this, he is calmly, indifferently waiting for his face to break apart and his eyes to turn into brine.

A surprised little smile flickers over Dean's lips and he looks at David with a funny look, perplexed. Dean's eyes are young, his forehead is youthful. His lips are loutish and full, but they look rather gentle right now. He smiles again, this time at David, *for* David, and his hand lifts to caress David's neck— Dean feels it trembling and thinks maybe the rubbing will make the shaking stop—and next, simply by making the gentleness of his touch become firmer, he starts to pull David's head toward the bouncing, stiff prick. This time, David relents.

This is what David sees: He sees the spread, hairy thighs, the tightened but still very large scrotum hanging into the cleavage of the crotch; he sees the red tip of the penis rising up toward him like the nose of a space ship drifting through nothing, toward the moon.

This is what David hears: He hears Dean's breathing, deep and audible and manly. He sees the hairy belly moving in the rhythm of life.

This is what David feels: He feels Dean's rough hand pushing him down.

Until the instant he opened his lips, David had never imagined, not even in fantasy, that it would be possible even to imagine doing what he is doing now. It is like discovering a sixth sense or a fourth dimension.

David jerks away: "No! No! No!" and that makes Dean mad. He grabs the cringing boy again: "Shut up," but then he repents, and becomes slightly gentler, saying, "Come on, kid—I'll blow you after. . . ."

David hears this sentence, but the words don't mean anything to him. He can't believe what he hears, and though he understands the sentence, he doesn't really hear it.

"Come *on*, man . . . *make* it . . . come *on* . . ." and Dean is pulling David down again so that David's straining, shaking back and neck fold over. David's lips open. His eyes close. After being battered for the past minute by some kind of whistly whir crashing inside his eardrum David's inner ear becomes still, and now his ears are gone. There is no sound. There is no light. The trembling in David's body has stopped and his nervous system seems to edge loose, break and float while his legs turn limber and soft, begin to fade, and now David finds himself without legs, without eyes, without a back, without arms, without lips, without a forehead, without cheeks, without eyebrows, and then he feels his own groin come alive and he can't hear Dean moaning while the rough flesh moves and strains, can't hear him cursing and hissing and beating his soft clenched big fists against David's bent back as if his fists were rolling drumsticks pounding on something dead.

Part Two

REMEMBER THIS: When the gusty, cool morning wind makes Harriet jump and wake up in the black leather chair, the first thing she sees is the bursting, depthless blue air, and her very first thought is about her lover, not about David. By the time Harriet wakes, David is lying safe, curled up, warm, asleep in his own bedroom below. Harriet arches her back—her back aches—and in the fantasy left over from sleep she sees the man's big face, his black hair flying and his brown eyes wild and contented with something he is doing. Something rough, pulling, jabbing, physical, even though she can't quite picture what it is. Then she remembers seeing the big column of his body twisting as he looked behind at something, she can't tell what. Everything about him seems to be fluttering with body happiness, stretching muscles that ripple, dark eyes. Harriet feels the gusty slap of the wind rushing through the open window and then feels her own hair tangled and blowing in it, and she grasps her hair. She stretches again —a long stretch to erase the aches—and then through the gaping window she sees the mound of green grass below, a rounded bump of grass in the morning light, and almost at the very same time she sees the tall grove and all its columns of blowing leaves, very bright and very green, and then she hears in the wind the fast swoop of some black crying birds.

Remember that David and Harriet live within the confines of a magic circle that each fills with an invisible light, visible only to the other. They bathe in this light, bathe in it alone. They cup it in their hands and warm their lips and cheeks with it; it makes their eyebrows wet; they let it pour down their chests and abdomens, dribbling down. They sink down into it, their knees rising up. They close their eyes. Everything is dark. They feel warm.

Remember that David and Harriet are the virtuous children of a dissolute generation who have raised each other on their own, unhelped but entirely protected. Their world has been this vast house—the dining rooms all mahogany with high-backed chairs like courtiers; the drawing room stretching a mile under dreary chandeliers, passing through clusters of furniture until it ends with a splash in a huge white marble fireplace that gapes as big as the gate to a palace; their own arching bedrooms; the grand entrance hall, dark with its reddish Victorian wood but also bright with the beveled mirrors that reach to the vaulted ceilings—and they fill the house. They are alone in it, and like something wet, their solitude overflows and spreads over that world like paint spilling from the can, until it covers the playhouse like an immense stain. The stain is a blanket. They sleep under it.

Their solitude emanates like radio beams that span the earth, or rather it did once. But as they grow stronger they also grow apart, and their world is dilating inward and turning the house into the space of four or five rooms—the only ones they ever think about or use—into a big lawn, a long hallway, the back of a limousine. The house and its rooms are boring.

Space is boring. David and Harriet have begun to feel restless, and instead of meeting each other immediately after school, never hesitating as they walk to the street corner where the limousine meets them—both of them surrounded by a glaring, quiet cloud of anger—now they glance out of the corner of their eyes as they walk; they see boys laughing, girls whose bodies are beginning to have a shape, breasts and thighs under the cloth. The walls of the house have become flat, painted, a bore; the air, which always seems to stink of furniture polish, is unendurable, like gas from a grave. David and Harriet have lost the ability to turn their dining room into a dark closet where they can crouch and hide together. The Royal Mission pitched at the outer reaches of the world has shrunk to the four walls of a few adult rooms, and it has become their prison. The watchmen have grown taller until they guard each other's cells. David and Harriet have stopped talking to each other; they have cut off their radio communication with the outer world, or rather it has fallen silent. They are restless, bored. Bored, scared.

Remember this: Remember your own buzzing, pestered unhappiness during adolescence and then freeze it. That will help. Remember being alone when you wake up suddenly in a strange place.

>

Harriet is down in her bedroom, looking very different than she did. After she came back from David's turret she took off her clothes and showered in cool water, sloughed off the wrinkled things and tried to rinse away the battered ache of a bad sleep. When she is dressed in fresh clothes her exhausted eyes feel darkened and raw. Harriet sits on a window sill, the curtain folded like a cushion at her back, and she is gazing in her placid morning manner down on the quiet green below. Even though she is alone, she is very conspicuously smoking a cigarette—tapping the ashes into a little sea-shell ashtray which she holds in the other hand—while the uncolored, bluish-gray smoke is very slowly sucked under the opened sash as if the window were a big gaping mouth, filling its lungs in a prolonged deep French inhale.

Harriet gags on a rough drag and coughs, coughs very loudly, twice, and closes her eyes. When the spasms are gone and she opens them again, the first thing she sees down below is David, walking across the lawn with his hands limp at his sides, watching the grass passing underneath his feet. He does not look up, and he is moving at an unchanging pace, quite slowly.

When Harriet looks at him she becomes rather nervous; she notices that her hand feels tingling as she lifts it for another drag, that it is almost trembling. In fact, she wants to step away. She suddenly must step away. Harriet stands. She has just become aware that she is very much afraid.

This is what she sees: She sees David's face, very close to hers, turning upward and looking at her window.

Harriet backs away, frowning, her heart is pounding, slamming, there is a wild, frightened voice inside her saying this: *Oh, my God, he'll see you, hide, Harriet, hide, oh, my God, get away, he'll see.* Harriet doesn't know what to do. She is crumbling under the pull of her fear, the voice inside her is getting strident, and terror is rising like a continuous urge, all her muscles harden, her legs get stiff and her backward walk away from the window grows clumsy and stops. *Oh, my God, he'll see you, hide, he'll see you.* Harriet's fist clamps shut, grinds into her cigarette so that it breaks and the red coal shatters, the sparks are rolling all over her fingers and she is battering the flying sparks with both hands, stamping on the floor, prancing in a soundless dance. For she doesn't make a sound. Her breath is still.

Now she flashes past the window and pins herself against the wall, presses her back into it. *Look at her face:* its terror like the terror of somebody in a movie pressed against a wall; Harriet is frozen as if she were pinned against the concentration camp wall, waiting for the white-hot finger of the searchlight to sweep by and stab her there, that killing, lethal beam soundlessly grinding by. Her terror is pulling all over Harriet, pulling all her muscles, her thighs. Her arms are pushing outward and the crown of her head is rolling against the wall.

This is what she sees: She sees her own body plummeting, ripped by a round from the Tommy guns and flung into the coiled barbed wire. She sees the huge negligent night eye passing over her where she crouches at the wall, missing her in its circling, futile, scooping night search, transfixingly brilliant, but blind.

➤

Look up there into Harriet's bedroom window. She just walked by, moving rather stiffly, looking prim. When she passed by the window she did not glance out, and now she has disappeared. Turn around. Did you hear that? Did you see that? David just closed the workshop door.

➤

Harriet's head is rolling in the cushioned back of her armchair. She feels like she wants to cry. Her hands are folded in

151

her lap, and her head rolls slowly back and forth. Notice that right now she is biting her lower lip, biting it hard; the skin is squeezed bloodless and white. She closes her eyes.

This is what Harriet sees: She is with her lover, holding his hand, and they are running together, far away, way out by the fence near the highway. Looking down on them from her bedroom window, Harriet can see both of them running, tiny figures in the darkness. They are near the rusted steel fence spears, bent where her lover squeezes through the fence each night to come and find her. Now he is taking her, they are leaving together; she crouches behind him, frozen and scared at the thought that they can be seen, they could be seen from the house if only somebody would look. Harriet is so frightened that she can only feel her lover's firm, warm hand. Harriet strains at the window, trying to pick out the two of them out there by the fence, so small that they are almost invisible. Harriet squints. She strains, looking through the glass. But the Harriet running is terrified: *who can see? who can see? can he see me now? can he? can he?* and she looks back at the house and its red sandstone hue is clearly perceptible even now, at night after every light is dead. Harriet feels like a character in a girl detective novel, she feels like Nancy Drew. *Can he see me now?* First her lover squeezes through the bent bars; when he gets through he holds out his hand and now she follows, but she takes a bit longer pulling through the aperture because she is sure that the spurs on the rusted steel fence will poke into her clothes and rip them. But now she's free. Once they are beyond the fence the dull shadows behind the fence are so obscure that Harriet can hardly make out the difference between the man and the woman, between the leader and the follower, or—now that one of them is running toward the car—the one who is running and the one still walking. Harriet hears a sharp, loud sound, as if it were amplified in a movie; it is the sound of a car door opening. Harriet hears a heavy, quick male hand flick the ignition key and she hears his foot hit the accelerator and she hears the engine roar. She can feel him cradling the stick in his palm. The man's weight shifts. There is a willful expression in his eyes, and she sees it as she sits beside him and the tires are pulling. They are squealing while the wild engine screams.

➤

In her chair, Harriet lets her face go in one long moan, and she doubles over, her folded arms clutching convulsively at her abdomen. Now she stops, pulls herself up straight. She doesn't make a sound. She looses her arms, pulls one hand through her hair. She closes her eyes, trying to get some peace.

This is what she sees: She sees herself lying on a mound of dry leaves and she sees her lover standing over her with his legs spread. His mouth is open and his shouting ramifies like rings spreading on still water. Harriet sees the man's body bending toward her; she knows that he is kneeling now. He seems like a king kneeling beside a soldier just about to die. Now the man is on top of her; his body is strong and large. It isn't young and the tough flesh is the flesh of middle age, a little battered, the soft skin gouged and healed. All of the man's weight is rolling on her. He is pressing his scratching beard against her so violently that she winces and wants to pull away; she slaps her hands on the small of his rough, hairy back; she both wants him and wants to shove him away. She still feels the rough pushing of his kiss against her face and out of the corner of her eye she sees his strong arms. But now the man seems to be drawing away, even though he is working his jaw, driven by the thrust of what he wants; his face is pulling away from her and she sees it sinking upward into the space above where she lies. He is gently vanishing at the same moment that his body is twisting with the impetuousness of his need. Smiling, Harriet turns her face away just as gently and then looks back at the moment when he at last disappears. Smiling again, she closes her eyes.

Harriet opens her eyes. The room is still, filled with the peaceful sunlight. She has decided what to do next just as her telephone rings.

⤝

Look in through the clean window pane, down there by the end of the workbench where David threw up last night. There he is again, crouching all alone, bending over with a look of fastidious disgust smeared across his face, his wincing features smearing, trying to twist away in loathing as he pries up the edges of the stiff, rotting rags still reeking. The mound of vomit is caking and almost dry. David folds the rags over onto each other, and he looks around the workroom for a trash can. Now he stands, glancing around; he is rummaging at the workbench, standing right before the window where we are looking in. Look at his face: his eyebrows are contracted and there is a look of irritation on his face; on the workbench a ball-peen hammer is lying on a piece of cardboard, and David shoves the hammer aside with a rough jab of his hand. The glue of some dried paint welds the cardboard to the workbench, and when David tries to lift the cardboard the paper rips in half, so David's annoyance grows sharper.

Now he turns his back to us. He spots a flat piece of scrap

plywood in a corner across the room. He walks to the corner, pulls it out, and carries the makeshift shovel back to the stinking pile, crouching while he slips it under the soggy rags, using it like a dust pan. Now he lifts the whole mess, and turning, looking away as he walks, he carries the foul pile to a garbage can in the corner near the door. He lifts the top, balancing the plywood like a tray, and now he dumps everything in, plywood and all. Now he pushes the top down hard. And pushes again. He turns back, his face relieved, and seems to look right at us.

Look at him there. His face clears, growing sweet again, its anxious disgust erased. There is almost a smile on it now.

David's eyes alight on the rickety wooden dog kennel where last night he became aware of Dean, stretched out and swearing. While he gazes at the empty place, a special kind of stillness settles over David; a stupid, utter narcosis makes his face go limp. His face sags and drops open, just as his lips drop open and hang a little. His mind is drained by what it sees on the spot.

This is what he sees: He sees the sprawling, stupid lout, just as he was last night—dirty, self-infatuated, wise-ass, hugging that blatant, ostentatious white helmet he never wears. Dean's mouth is turned in a nasty smirk; he is rocking on his butt a little; he is snickering a low, long continuous snicker—quiet, solely for his own pleasure—and it makes that tight, muscular belly of his move in easy, relaxed spasms, and his eyes are self-satisfied and happily mocking while he lies there. He is laughing at this: that poor, weak, terrified, frail kid bent over, huddled at the end of the workbench, his weak, white, bony hand—still a little boy's hand, but white now like an old man's

—gripping the concrete urn while the puke splashes and gushes, pouring from his stinging mouth as if it would never stop. Standing in the center of the room, David watches the image rock and laugh. David's mouth hangs open. He is breathing loudly through his mouth. Dean is smirking at the spectacle, scratching his guts near his navel.

This is what David sees: He sees a picture from last night, bathed in black light, an image drawn in blue cloth of Dean standing with his thumbs stuck into his big belt while he stands in a haunchy contrapposto at the window, confidently looking out into the darkness. David sees Dean turning around to look at him. David can see his face in the light now, and there's a filthy smile on it, a leer. David is aware of Dean's going and his genitals folded into the thick, dirty blue denim.

➞

Take a look at David's real face, over there, in the sunlight where he stands. David is scared, and he has forgotten himself. His features are bewildered, like those of a little boy in a crowd.

He rubs his hands on his sides. He grips his sides. He walks to the kennel and tests its edge with his fingertips, and now he turns to hoist himself onto it, and now there he sits with his feet dangling. As they move around the room, his eyes check out enemy ground, hardly daring admit that they see only the empty workroom, the cluttered workbench scattered with paint and tools, the rough planking on the walls, the lawn mowers and garden furniture falling apart, the dirty windows. But the room is empty. David's eyes keep restlessly moving from corner, to wall, to floor.

And his hands have begun to move, to lightly touch his own

thighs. He is rubbing, caressing them. Now his jumpy finger-tips move even higher and press, test his genitals. David seems to be glancing around to make sure that nobody is watching. Now he cups his crotch in his hands.

He won't masturbate. David pulls his hands away and leans all his weight on his two elbows so that he is lying back with his legs spread. His eyes are blank and stare straight in front of him. They close. Now he shifts his weight so that he is resting on one elbow and looking more like the sexy, sneering lout he is remembering vaguely, but suddenly his body shudders once and he abruptly sits up again. He stands, and in a spasm clasps both hands to his face and pushes into them, rocking his head as if he were hysterical, rocking in pain, but when they fly apart and expose his face once more his features are entirely without any expression. Look at David's fluttering hands: now they are rubbing slowly and deeply in his groin, not touching his genitals, but massaging the brown cloth around the tops of his thighs. His blank eyes suddenly fill and he is looking from wall to wall, spot to spot, desperately, harshly, his eyes flicking, and now he seems to jump, jump in terror, and his flailing arms flick around him like two ropes whipping around a post, and with a face in anguish he is hugging himself, rocking himself, bending himself back and forth while an expression snaps across his face like that of a child playing cops and robbers, pretending he's just been shot—*they got me, they got me, they got me in the guts, I've been hit—hit! hit!*—and pretty soon he'll be tumbling, flipping all over himself like a blasted rabbit on the frozen ground. His arms are still embracing his own torso and still rocking in the wild, harsh, soothing rhythm. The expression on David's face clears. He drops his hands. He again sits on the edge of the kennel and hoists himself onto it. He reclines again. Again his eyes are void.

✳

Harriet is curled on the bed, tucked on her side while she dandles the phone against her belly and cocks her head, folding the receiver into her shoulder so her cheek is its cushion and her lips make the black plastic mouthpiece wet. Harriet can taste it on her lips. The voice speaking to her from New York is scratching and clicking every few seconds, telling her that he wants to do it outside again tonight, it turns him on that way. Now the phone pick-up of his voice is becoming sexual, a voice curling inside the earpiece, folding over Harriet's ear, and as it comes out Harriet punctuates it with mechanical Yes's repeated at regular, rather long, lazy intervals. But none of his words are reaching her; all she hears is a voice scratching inside a phone receiver, interrupting her solitude and saying something which doesn't need to be said. The voice is saying the obvious, she is assenting to the obvious—it is all so natural and dull. It will all be outside again, he wants it outside, that really gets to him, all the darkness and the fresh breeze, daring to stand naked out in the open like that, all in the vast, black, wild seclusion of a very rich girl's lawn, it's really too much, a bang so delicate it knocks him out—lays him out—but of course he doesn't say a word of this now. He is saying the obvious; Harriet is assenting to the obvious, even though the sound of his voice is a bore, interrupting her—a raid on her territory, a sneaky way of jumping across the forbidden lines, electronically, on a wire. She does not sense her lover out *there*—wherever he is, in a phone booth, in his office, in his apartment on the East Side of Manhattan, calling from the back of a bar or a laden, gleaming delicatessen somewhere.

158

She feels only that his voice is here, at her ear, she has to hold it there and that's a drag, it hurts, she hates it. Listening to someone else partly erases her. To keep herself from disappearing entirely she keeps emitting the vapid verbal nods of hers, Yes. Yes. Yes. Yes. Yes.

This is what Harriet sees: She sees her lover's large hand, heavily flesh-colored and warm, reaching toward her, about to touch her breasts. She sees his face looking at her. It seems very far away, and wild.

Suddenly Harriet interrupts the electronic tickle of his voice. Now she takes it back, she doesn't want to meet him outside tonight, she wants him to come up here to her bedroom.

"Because? Well, just because. I just don't want to be out there again tonight, that's all. I'd rather meet you so we could come up here, here to my room. Here in the house."

But will that work? Won't somebody find out? Won't somebody see us? No. No. No. They won't be seen. But are you sure? Won't the aunt get wind of something? No. No. No. O.K. O.K. Fine. Goodbye.

With a groan and a heft, Harriet lunks the telephone into the Chippendale chair, then rolls onto her stomach and rests her head in her folded arms. The thought of David suddenly reminds her that she had decided to see him. Harriet rolls onto her back. She sits. She stands.

On the way downstairs, it doesn't occur to her that David might want to be left alone or that she might be intruding on something. She feels completely certain of something that is utterly unformed in her mind, elated in her certainty about nothing. She'll spy. She'll sneak. Everything about her feels light, so she can run down the grand staircase fast, her feet moving faster than her eyes could ever follow, moving like flashes of white, and she is gliding as easily as a movie star flying down the stairs, deliciously happy, going as fast as she can go and feeling like a real woman doing it, fast like a star. She flashes across the broad empty entryway, and then she's gone.

By now Harriet is outside, creeping along the wall of the chalet, afraid she will catch her blouse on a splinter in the rough stained wood and noticing the gravel strewn around the little building's foundation. She is tiptoeing, walking sideways, looking out toward the rear fence and opening and closing her eyes with each step until now, just now, she reaches that window with the clean pane. She stops and freezes; the thrill of the window's being so near has touched her, and now she is poking her insides with the prod of her will, trying to push loose the little animal of nerve that will make her turn to it and look. David is inside, she knows he is; she tries to imagine him in there, but it's hard. Every time she tries she sees nothing, imagines nothing. Once again she is trying very hard to picture him and her exaggeration finally makes her shake her head and turn to the window pane.

This is what she sees: David is really inside there all right, she finds him right away, back in the shadowy part of the room sitting on a battered old kennel like a big crate, with his feet dangling loose. His feet are not quite touching the dirty, paint-spattered concrete floor. Something is wrong; Harriet is forcing herself onto tiptoes and she sees David doubled over on himself, his face is squeezed into his hands. He is rocking back and forth. He seems to be hurting. David looks like a Kitschy statue, the hokey incarnation of Anguish, the hewn-

160

wood figure of Despair. His face is covered: Harriet can see his hands, he is pressing hard. When he drops them into his lap with his fingers all limp, the face he uncovers shows no expression at all.

But his face still makes Harriet jump. *Get back*, the voice whispers inside her, *get back, he'll see.* She presses her back against the wall, and she is looking out toward the fence again. She moves delicately, cautiously this time, her features terrified, certain her brother got a glimpse of her. Real terror is banging inside her again, but tempered by reality this time, subsumed in the long chance that it might be justified. The scared girl holds still a long time, her face withheld, made stately and serene by the freeze of that dangerous possibility. Harriet holds still longer than it would take to tell about it. Harriet rubs her hand across her mouth again, calmly and loosely, and once more turns to look.

This is what she sees: Once more David has hunched over and buried his face. Harriet notices an old, absurdly narrow, rusted lawn mower hanging from a hook on the far wall. David is slowly rocking back and forth like a Talmudic student at his desk, still pressing his face into his hands. Harriet can't hear a thing.

There isn't any sound inside at all, nothing except the regular, high-pitched creaks of wood repeated in the steady rhythm of David's motion.

Now Harriet sees him uncover his face again. His gaze is once more blank. Once more his lower lip hangs. David is breathing through his mouth, making a certain kind of sound. *Listen:* there is the suck of saliva. He coughs. Suddenly he clutches his arms again, rocks in his own embrace, and now limply lets his hands fall to his thighs, and he lightly caresses his thighs a few times before he closes his hand over his crotch. He squeezes his face shut. He bends down.

> ↣

Harriet silently claps her left hand over her mouth and spins away. Not that. She never even thought of that. She is looking out toward the highway, but she doesn't see it. Her distress freezes, recedes. Mechanically, placidly, she turns and looks in through the window again.

This is what Harriet sees: David has begun to massage his groin with his hands, one hand after the other as if he were playing scales at the piano, feeling and testing the bulge in the cloth, his lips hanging open, his eyes blinking but seeing nothing, staring straight ahead somewhere toward the edge of the workbench.

This is what David sees: He sees a boy's white hand gripping the concrete urn. He hears the loutish laughter. He sees the shower of slime.

David has spread his legs, and once or twice he winces rather visibly. A couple of times he rolls his wrist against his forehead, like somebody in an old advertisement, a woman with wet hands, exhausted by working over her wooden tub. David's hand crawls back to his thigh. He is listening to his own short little grunts, they excite him, they turn him on, his own sound, moans that Harriet can't hear.

David leans back a little on the wood. The fingers of his right hand are slithering underneath his waistband, they are touching hair.

Harriet's hand is squeezing her lips hard. She has got to

162

look away, got to. She stares down at the ground, sees the pebbles at her feet. She closes her eyes. She releases her face and shakes her head back and forth very hard. Her hair slaps her cheeks. She wants to look up again.

This is what she sees: David's probing hand is pulling out from his pants, not touching the warm skin any more. He bounces, shifts his weight, rolls his wrist on his forehead again and then suddenly his face snaps into a new, hard expression. His fingers seem to flutter in a fingery blur at his belt buckle. He pulls it loose. It hangs. David's hand is against his skin, savoring its softness, soaking in it, pressing toward his hidden pubic hair. Harriet can see his hand moving downward again and again, groping in a tentative, repetitive way like a hand looking for soap in the bottom of a bathtub. And now Harriet suddenly can see the skin of David's wrist, a whole big band of it coming clear, and she desperately wants to look away. Her hand is still clapped over her mouth as if it were trying to force her to turn her head, force her to stop looking, obey her sterile impulse, but it isn't going to work, she can't stop, her hand is pressing against her but she can't stop.

This is what she sees: She sees absolutely nothing at all. She sees some strange man's face laughing at her, each one of his big features very clear: His mouth. His eyes. His hair. His teeth.

This is what she sees: David hoists his own weight up an inch or two in order to slip his pants down. They slip halfway down his thighs. They are held by his spread knees. Harriet can see all the naked flesh of David's hips. She sees the top of the black pubic hair.

Harriet's fists clench very tightly. Her mouth moves. Her jaw keeps moving back and forth. Sometimes her teeth scrape.

This is what she sees: She sees the black, curling crown of pubic hair, an immense amount, much more than she has, more than she could ever have imagined. It shocks her: she has seen David naked, but that was before he had any pubic hair at all. In a moment he will turn in such a way that she will see his penis. It is growing erect. And now she sees it, sees its tip, sees it all, swelling and dark, dark like the hair and large, and it makes her stomach jump. Harriet is wincing. Her clenched fingernails grind into her palms. Her mouth is moving in a strange, tight, meaningless way. In one more instant, Harriet will see a picture, a picture of herself. It will flash in front of her faster than the time it takes to blink.

This is what she sees: She sees her own face, covered with blood, faceless.

David's hands are caressing his thighs, squeezing them. He moves his weight back and forth, and his mouth hangs. Harriet sees the flesh of his legs sinking under his fingertips. She keeps trying to look away. Her hand has dropped away from her mouth. Now David cups his testicles in his palm and fondles them. His mouth hangs open and his eyes close. He leans back, half reclining, and now he has begun to roll on his side, and suddenly Harriet can see the crevice of his buttocks.

➤

Harriet has turned away, and all her shame is rising up to crush her. It is going to strike her down. Her desecrated eyes are wild, they see nothing but the bleary green, they are blinking in a hysteria of loathing. She is dropping, she is sinking,

sinking to her knees. Her knees touch the ground, they press into the crushed stones scattered around the foundation of the chalet, pinching and stabbing her tender kneecaps like little bits of shattered steel. Harriet is making some kind of sound, and there is a look of exaggerated anguish on her face. Upright on her knees, like a penitent, Harriet walks, crawls across the rocks, until she reaches the cool, soft border of grass, where she falls into an unsupported mound, her head on her arms, her head turning in an odd, self-comforting, spasmodic way.

Look at her. Look at the way her lips are moving. Harriet is desperate in her shame. She is trying to wail in a whisper. *Listen to her:* "Oh God. Oh Davy. Oh God, what am I doing? What am I doing? What if he saw me? Oh God"—but now her words veer down, die into some unarticulated sound. *Listen again:* Harriet has put her hand over her eyes. She feels the soft grass gently pricking her calves, cooling her skin, and with her free hand she brushes away some sand that still clings to her knees. *Listen: Oh, my God, Davy. I've got to stop myself. Oh, my God. I've got to stop myself. What if he saw me? What if he saw me?*

Harriet sits up, straight, upright. All the wide green, the columned, shaded expanse around her, contracts into her decision, her willfulness. Harriet brushes her palms against each other, fast and noiselessly. Every inch of her face is still and frigid. She stands, and standing, the upright column of her body snaps to. She walks directly to the corner of the building, narrowly skirting a clump of bridal wreath, and bounds under the heavy canopy of the main door. She knocks very loudly five times and then is silent.

Now she shouts: *Davy? Open up! It's me!*

She knocks again, but differently, the rapping flutters gently, too often to count.

David, please open up. Hey, hurry up, it's me.

Not a sound inside.

David? Not a sound. *Davy?* A pause. *Open up, hey, please?* There is a long pause. *I know you're in there, Davy, I saw you go in.* Harriet stops to listen again, and once again hears silence. She turns her back to the door. She closes her eyes.

This is what she sees: She sees a picture of something torn in half by two big hands.

She blinks.

This is what she sees: She sees a color television screen breaking into prisms smeared with red and yellow. She sees the colored tube burst with a gasp, and a spray of electronic confetti come scattering onto the rug.

This is what she sees: She sees water splashing, splashing against a glass that keeps her dry.

Harriet spins on her heel and starts slamming the door as hard as she can. *Davy!* You open up this door right now, do you hear?

Damn you! Harriet does not hear herself say this. She whispers the curse under her breath. *God damn you, David!* Harriet is deaf to herself. GOD DAMN YOU, DAVID. It is a whisper. OPEN. OPEN. OPEN. OPEN.

Harriet turns and leans again. She looks across the lawn and notices the garage doors directly across the way, serene like three big hanging canvases. Cool. Secure. ABC.

Harriet closes her eyes. *This is what she sees:* Flecks of

colored light dance behind her eyelids. She thinks she is about to cry.

She turns again, more slowly this time. She lifts her fist to knock again but she hesitates. She knocks again about four times, and suddenly she jumps when she hears David's footsteps coming very gently toward the closed door. She can hear them even though they come so quietly and slowly.

>―

When David opens the door, he sees first Harriet's trembling anger and her eyes almost in tears. David backs away from the girl in the doorway, bends in an exaggerated bow as if to usher her into the shop. He has jammed his hands into his trouser pockets. Harriet looks at her brother. There is no smile on his face. She does not notice that his lips are trembling, but she does see that his skin is splotched with splashes of red.

Harriet is standing in the room with her back turned toward him.

"So," David says after a very long interval. He clears his throat. "What's the big hurry? Can't you leave me alone? Is the house on fire or something?" Harriet notices that his voice trembles a little.

Harriet passes her hand across her face, clutches the hair at the top of her head, and produces a stagy moan. She twitches her spine and turns to look into those vacated eyes of his, black and cruel in their rage.

"Oh, I just wanted to come in and see you just for a few minutes, Davy, that's all. I really didn't mean to make you mad. I just wanted to see you. . . ."

"Well, damn it, leave me alone. I just want to be left alone." David is amazed by his own precision, his ability to say what he wants without losing control or squeaking or gagging. "Just leave me alone." And now, in contradiction to his own words, he carries his control still further, turns away and firmly slams the heavy door shut.

Look in through the window. Harriet with her back to us, facing David, her arms folded by this time, David's face in full view, directly in our line of vision. His full lips are moving rapidly, precisely, and with great strength. He is speaking so loudly that we can almost hear him.

Listen: "Just who the hell do you think you are, anyway, barging in on me just because I am out here alone, who do you think you are, just because you're my sister. Damn you. Leave me alone. When I want to see you you'll know. Who in hell do you think you are?"

Harriet has never heard David use profanity. Each time she winces. She can hardly believe what she hears. *"Who the hell. Damn you."* This is her little brother. She is shocked.

And David begins to pace. "Like just who the *hell*? Don't I deserve my privacy, huh? Don't I deserve my privacy? Have I ever bothered you before? Huh? Have I ever?" He thinks his voice sounds like a man's.

Harriet's head is bowed. David has walked around her—she does not turn—so that now he is pacing behind her, along the workbench. David glances out the window. Now he looks at her back and really shouts: *"Leave me alone, see?"*

After a long pause, Harriet finally speaks, still without turning around. She uses a trembly, low, calculating voice.

"How come you closed the door, Davy? Huh? Why?"

David stops still, then pivots to lean into both hands pressed against the workbench. *Oh, my God.* He picks up a screwdriver and begins to spin it in his grip. "How come I closed the door?" He laughs two or three times, his head rolling in feigned sarcastic dismay. "Why, why? Because I wanted to be alone, is it such a big secr—"

"No. No." Harriet interrupts him. "I mean how come you closed the door just *now?* Not when you came in, but just *now.*"

David stops spinning the screwdriver and holds it still. "What?"

As Harriet turns, her face has been made more gentle, but her voice still trips over a little quavering accent of fear as she confronts him. "I said how come you closed the door just now? I mean when I came in here just now."

"Close the door?" David glances at the door. "I don't know." This word is weak and quiet. David has just disappeared, gone somewhere else, but he comes back, he can regain his rage now. "I don't know, don't be so stupid, Harriet, I don't know, who *cares?* You must be *craaazy.*" The epithet comes through his teeth, a hiss of adolescent mockery. "*Craaazy.* So *what* if I closed the door?"

"Oh, Davy, shut *up.*" The wail comes while Harriet paces in exasperation.

"Shut up yourself."

"Oh, please, please, just shut *up.*"

David's back is again turned toward his sister; he is leaning on the workbench with one hand, using the palm of his free hand to roll the handle of the screwdriver on the bench top, but now he shoves it away, glances up out the window again, and closes his eyes. "Christ," he says. He is slowly shaking his head. "Christ."

"Oh, Davy." Harriet speaks in a soft voice, trying to mimic a motherly sound, something gentle and giving. "I'm sorry I came in. I didn't think. I had to. I just couldn't help it. I just couldn't help looking. I'm sorry."

David freezes absolutely still. He has been rocking his weight into the edge of the workbench, but now he is utterly still.

Harriet is looking at her brother's bent back, the slump of his shoulders propping his leaning weight. She hears him muttering, perceives his exasperation, feels his body begin to recede from her and disappear, senses it pulling away the way a motorcycle passes a slowly moving car, its sound diminishing. She gets a glimpse of the black curled hair on the back of her brother's neck, just where his trapezius muscle rises to vanish.

"Oh, Davy." She speaks again in a low, soft moan, trying to bring him back. "Oh, Davy, I'm sorry. I really am. I mean I really didn't mean to, Davy. I didn't. I just couldn't help it, I didn't even think, I just couldn't help it. I'm sorry, I'm . . ."

But David is dead to her, unmoving, utterly still, frozen. Her voice seems to be breathing right at his ear, but he won't turn his head. The weight on his arms bears down, inert. A moment ago, he was nervously aware that too much saliva was rolling around in his mouth, sliding over his flabby tongue. Now he forgets it and his lips seem to be erased, wiped away. He isn't seeing a thing even though his frozen eyes stare.

Suddenly he is afraid that he is going to drool, slobber onto the screwdriver, onto the floor. His knees are getting weak, they are giving beneath him, he is afraid, there is a pain in his chest.

"Oh, Davy, I'm sorry."

David is standing there trying to make the universe contract. Look in through the window. There he is, his closed eyes squeezing convulsively, his tight, squirming lips pulling against each other. He stands right where he was a minute ago, still filling the whole space, but he is shrinking inside like the incredible shrinking man; he is riding a roller-coaster into his own minuscule image of shame, squirming safe inside the dead big body that surrounds him like a colosseum. David's hands are pressing so hard into the edge of the table that it seems to be cutting them, but David feels nothing at all. But now that safety of littleness is over, he returns to himself, pops back to size and remembers where he is, feeling Harriet behind him, feeling her female pout and her sad, evocative voice pronouncing that seductive denunciation that fills him up with crawling shame, "Oh, Davy, I'm sorry, I'm so sorry . . ." but the space around where he is standing is dilating inward like a TV screen turned out, the extinguished field sinking into one last lingering point of white light. Behind his eyes, David sees nothing at all.

That stasis is over now, David can't take any more, he is going to fall. Look in through the window at his face falling apart, looking as if he would start sobbing; his knees are giving way and now he sinks down kneeling, he feels himself going and he can't stop it. "Oh, no, no," he begins to say. "Oh, my God, oh, no, no, no . . ."

Harriet stops looking at David's neck when his knees break and he starts making those sounds. Her hands are hanging at her sides. She is rubbing her thumbs very lightly against her fingertips. She is almost holding her breath.

David is making a very loud sound now.

"Oh, no," he is saying. "Oh, no, I want to die, I don't want to be alive, I want to die. Oh, no, no, no, no . . ." He is searching for a rhythm that will soothe him, make him grow warm inside again. "Oh, no," he keeps saying. "I don't want to be alive."

In an instant Harriet is beside him, kneeling beside him herself; her knees are on stone again and she is tugging ineffectually at her brother's elbow. *Davy, Davy.* She glances up and takes a long firm glance out the window. Her eyes have an expression which makes them appear to be tear-filled, but look at them: they are perfectly dry.

Harriet turns to him again. *"Davy, Davy."* She is tugging much more gently now with both her hands, and he does not look up. "Oh, Davy, I'm sorry, dear, I really am," and now she very awkwardly extends her hands to the workbench top, stretching, fumbling for her brother's folded fists. *Davy, Davy.* They won't move, and so she lets her hands fall, her weight breaks, and both palms are pressing the cold floor so that she is on all fours, *oh, I'm so sorry,* and now she is upright again and her trembling girl's hand is touching her brother's hair, the touch is gentle, and she feels it, it is a boy's hair she is touching with the same fingertips with which an instant ago she was feeling her own gently caressing thumb. I'm so sorry.

With the tender touch, David rips loose his hands and tries to shove his sister's wrist away from his neck, striking it down as if her lingering hand were an animal that had dropped from the ceiling onto his back. "Cut it out," he gasps at her, and she stupidly replies with her mechanical tenderness, with her *oh,*

Davy, and with that he can't take any more and he hits for real. Harriet feels the stinging slap of David's partly open fist and she instantly shouts, "David! *Quit* it, that *hurts!*" but David isn't going to quit it, he is going to hit her again, and hit harder this time. His face is utterly red; his lips are taut and his eyes are narrowed. Still kneeling, grabbing a leg of the workbench with one hand for balance, he hits her with the skittering free one and the punch connects, really slams into her. It's not the blow but the sickening sound of it that makes Harriet want to scream; she hears her own cheek bashed inside her head and she won't feel the pain until a few minutes from now, when she'll feel the pain, feel lots and lots of pain. David is moaning through his teeth, and both his hands are down now. He is propped on all fours like an ape, and his fist is grinding into the floor. He looks into Harriet's face with his bulging, outraged eyes, and his lips moving. *You get away from me, you Goddamned bitch—don't you touch me!* The execration streams from his mouth in a scream that slashes into Harriet most violently of all. David's fist is grinding the floor and his eyes are burning. *You get the fucking hell away from me, you Goddamned bitch. You leave me alone, you leave me alone.* He screams still, his face blasted red, spit flailing in strings out of his mouth, and he doesn't see it, doesn't feel it, he sees only her, her, blasted and bewildered.

This is what he sees: Harriet's mouth hangs open, her arms hang straight at her sides, her mouth grows red as if lipstick had been smeared on it to look like blood. Her eyes connect with his, like his seeing nothing except their own amazement and rage.

David slaps again, and then he slaps again and the slap

cracks out loud, makes you hear it, it splits the air. David doesn't feel a thing on his palm except the sudden quick flash against the amazed flesh. It feels gentle almost, touched only by the contact's fast snap.

He hits her again. Harriet moves now, she falls down, rolls onto her side while she is pulling her hands over her head, pressing her elbows inward to protect her cheeks and shoulders, and so since her arms are helpless her tumbling body seems to hit the concrete with a kind of thud, but silently. David doesn't hear a thing.

David leaps up, both hands moving fast and loose, and he is pacing away from her, over by the door. Harriet's body, even though she is no longer physically threatened, is rocking on the floor, and David is shouting out loud:

"You bitch. You damned bitch. Why don't you go back to him and have a good happy time fucking it up, huh? God damn you, why don't you go, you pervert, you witch, you're crazy, that's what you are, so why don't you go into town and do it in the middle of the street, you pervert, why don't you get a TV show so you can fuck on TV. *You keep your damned hands off me, you bitch!*"

On her stomach, Harriet keeps pulling her hands down over her head, still holding up her weight on her elbows. Her eyes are wide open. Her hands seem to be trying to cover her ears where she cringes, but Harriet hears what is being said to her all right, it is all so obvious and inevitable, and so absolutely disconcerting and unexpected. She is looking at the floor.

This is what she sees: She sees the floor's dirty, sandy gray concrete and one wiggling crack squiggling across it, with a single grain of sand wedged into its abyss.

This is what Harriet sees: She sees David's distant hands flailing toward her. She sees the blank floor.

This is what she sees: She sees David's violent hands closing around her neck while she lies on the cool green ground. She sees the heels of her tennis shoes clawing, gouging into the grass. She sees herself crying.

This is what Harriet hears: "Davy! Davy! Be quiet, quick, come here! I can hear him! I can hear him! It's the King!"

This is what Harriet hears: "So why don't you lay out for him in the town square, you pervert . . . why don't you get a TV show so he can suck your cunt on TV . . . you crazy whore . . . do it for everybody to see, you bitch . . . you bitch . . . *you keep your hands . . .*"

Harriet rolls, she sits up, she stands, and now she is shouting.

Listen to her: "Stop, David, you don't know what you're talking about, you stop, you just be quiet and shut up, you leave *me* alone, you don't know what you're talking about . . ."

She shrieks, but not even a shriek can silence him.

"Yeah? Why don't you go out on the lawn to fuck with your pervert boy friend, that's what you want, isn't it? So why don't you go out and get it, why don't you if that's what you want, go out and fuck out there, it's what you want, isn't it? Isn't it? Huh?"

Harriet is pacing, crying too violently to see anything any more, her eyes all water, her cheeks, her lips, wet everywhere; she tastes the wet salt; she doesn't know what she is seeing or saying any more, she knows only what she keeps hearing. Harriet staggers to the workbench and picks up a hammer—it

175

is that ball-peen hammer. The rusted, narrow lawn mower hangs on the wall behind her. Her brother's hectoring voice continues: "You whore . . . you whore . . . you witch . . . go back to him . . . go back to your pervert boy friend," and all through the long diatribe Harriet keeps talking. Once her own voice almost veers into a shriek, she is shouting too, she is accusing, damning, sobbing, begging, refusing, but she can't hear her own words, she doesn't know what they say or where they come from (the low, light wooden dog kennel is over there behind her, in the shadows). Harriet looks directly out the window with her eyes filled by the tears that make her whole face gleaming wet; we can hardly see her eyes now; she glances upward—her lips are moving, she is speaking hysterically—she looks down, she is looking across the whole expanse of the workbench (the urn is on the floor, about five feet to her left), feeling across it like a blind woman with both her trembling hands, and she is speaking.

Listen to her, we'll hear even if she doesn't, if he doesn't: "Oh, please, leave me alone . . . I've never done anything wrong . . . oh, please leave me alone, I've never done anything wrong, you don't know what you're talking about . . . oh, please, Davy, you don't know . . ." and her hand brushes across the handle of the hammer, her hand gropes for it, grips it, picks it up, look at it rising up in her hand, lifting it way above her head and look at her face flashing into rage as she slams it down, smashing.

"NO!" The deep dent splinters its edge.

"NO!" She slams the hammer down again. "NO!" Again. "NO!" Again. "NO!" The shouting, the slamming have made David silent, and now the hammer slams down sideways, not on its head, and it almost bounces out of her hand, makes her gripping palm sting, sing, and now she swings it back another time, way backward over her shoulder, back so far that it looks as though the whipping iron head is going to strike the base of her spine, and then it flashes forward, flashes out of her hand, flipping over on itself halfway (but so fast that you never saw it), twisting its own flailing weight only halfway before the head hits the window pane, explodes the cross of wood within the crashing glass so that the sound of it deletes her own shriek, and now, now outside the hammer streaks outward across into the lawn like a flopping blasted steel fragment thrown by a bomb, while behind it is all the exploding broken glass all of it scattering, a thousand shattering fragments flying, blowing outward, raining their ice into a few square feet of the stupid summer green.

⤜

Look inside again. Harriet has turned toward her brother, the tears still pouring.

"Oh, Davy," she is saying, desperately. "Oh, Davy. Oh, please, please be quiet now. Oh, Davy, I hate you so much. Oh, please be quiet now."

David has frozen still. He sees every move his sister makes, the precision of his observation has become absolute, he sees each gesture, each move, his ears pick up each minute intonation, each tiny change. He is thinking about nothing at all.

Harriet's knees are weakening, her hip is bending outward, it touches the edge of the workbench, her eyes have begun to connect with his again and to implore him, and her voice keeps making noise in the silence: *Oh, Davy, please be quiet now. Oh, I hate you so much. Oh, please be quiet now. Oh, please . . .*

Harriet's hand is touching the edge of the workbench, near her hip. The tears continue; they keep coming.

Oh, Davy, Davy . . .

David begins to move toward her, both his hands hanging loose, hanging like an ape's hands. His eyes have stopped seeing. *Look at his face*: it is absolutely red, the blush of his rage is absolute.

Oh, Davy. Both David's hands are swinging back and forth, once he lets one fist slap into another palm, and now both hands are swinging free again. David has kicked the urn, stumbles into it with both feet and stubs the middle toes on his left foot so they hurt but he doesn't notice it, so without once looking down, without once in any way registering the pain on his face, without changing his posture or once changing the displacement of his weight, his lunging weight, he passes it, steps over it, and now that he is so much closer he starts hitting with both hands; he is still too far actually to strike her but both his hands are flailing, both hands moving in helpless arcs of rage, both half-closed fists describing flashing circles the way a windmill strikes the air. The spattering barrage of hands has begun to hit Harriet's face and her shoulders and her breasts and her hair and her neck, the hands spattering against her like a barrage of fifty hands at once, and even though Harriet is screaming David doesn't make a single sound.

This is what Harriet sees: She sees David's face in the middle distance, moving in spasmodic jerks, squeezed tight in its weeping, its eyes looking everywhere except at her.

Harriet raises her elbows again, just the way she did before, but she is standing this time and it is too late, he hit her nose and it's bleeding now, blood is pouring over her upper lip, and now another slap smears it into her cheek and it is all over her hands, she can't believe how much there is. She screams all the louder, her hands are down, she is going to fall, she has to, she screams all the louder, and what words are there for it, it's a sound you have never heard anywhere, a sound from the back wards, it is bleeding Harriet's wail of terror, listen to it, listen to her.

She falls and in an instant David has leapt on top of her, kneeling on her, and when the shriek subsides David lifts both his own hands and digs his nails into his own cheeks while his sister's blood furrows the lines. He sits on her. He won't let her go, no, not even if she blesses him. She is not looking at him now, her eyes are closed and turned aside. The tears squeeze without stopping between the closed slits, and the back of her hand, that hand which was so violent a moment ago, is pressed against her bleeding nostril, and it covers her lips, covers the terrible sound that keeps coming out of them.

Stunned, wordless, David keeps pulling his nails across his cheeks, he kneels with his spread legs over his sister, he is trying not to feel her crying, trying not to feel the spasms of her sobs under him, and he feels now exactly as he did when he slumped at the workbench at first, when he knelt in his shame the first time, but he feels it now for real, and the same words have come back, though he doesn't say them, he stays still: *Oh, my God, I want to die. Oh, my God, I don't want to live any more. Oh, my God, I want to die*, but for all the violence of these sentences heaving in the sterile silence of his mind, they are not going to still the hurting, violent girl underneath him, and not going to bring him to that banal One Thing Needful, the consummation of his shame in tears.

"Oh, my God, I don't want to live any more. I want to die.

179

I don't want to live, I want to die." Look at David's hands, scraping into his cheeks, wiping his sister's blood away, his eyes staring. "Oh, my God." But you can't hear anything, the words speak inside him, his lips don't move, his dead eyes merely stare: "Oh, my God . . . I . . . I . . . I . . . I . . . I . . ."

And now all the sounds stop, even inside his mind. He rolls off his sister, he kneels beside her, and when he touches her shoulder, she jerks away and won't look at him. Now it is David's turn to crawl like a penitent. He backs away from Harriet as she sits up—sits up pressing, testing her nostril with the back of her hand—and when she is sitting straight, David stops moving, slumps and sits, turns away from her and fixes his eyes on the floor.

The bleeding has stopped. The tip of Harriet's nostril is dry. She will not look at her brother. She is fumbling instead in a pocket of her dress, and now she pulls out a wad of Kleenex. She presses it on her lip, touches her nose with it. She is wiping herself clean. With her fingernail she gently flakes loose the patches of dried blood, and soon her face is relatively clean. Her left cheek hurts very much.

The voice inside David is jammed: his whole soul is held congealed in the homeostasis of shame.

Harriet wants only to stand up and get out, to leave the room as quickly as possible.

David looks up at her only once. He wishes that he didn't have to glance at her, but he can't help it. Harriet is sitting with her arms on her knees. She is looking at her hands. She is very still.

Harriet reaches up, pulls at the workbench, and rises.

David is not going to look at her again. He is staring at the floor, and he can't turn away. His face is unrecognizably distorted, and his posture is like Narcissus at the pool, except that David is conscious only of the world outside his field of vision, conscious only of the blank, black landscape utterly filled with one person whom he does not see.

Very gently, Harriet closes the door.

➤

And, when it has closed, that blank landscape is filled with a tense, sexual silence. It grips the room and holds David in it, squeezes him perfectly still. David feels his own weight on his hands. He is aware of his own expression of anguish, caked around his face like mud. He shifts his weight and drops, so he can bury his head in his arms. Now David will try to enact the desperate emotions that he can almost feel going through him at this moment. Perfectly still, jammed up inside, he feels that his remorse is almost violent. Look in at him through the window. He is sprawling there, rolling very slightly on the floor. He moves his head back and forth on his arms. He is almost certainly moaning. The shame of what he has done is unbearable, and he is trying to make himself feel it as such, but he isn't going to succeed. His shame is so intense that he can't unlock it and make it real. It is going to die.

Now he stops moving, and lies perfectly still on the dark concrete with his head on his arms. He might be sunning himself on a beach in the baking sun, asleep. And now in his stillness David sees something wiggling behind his eyes.

This is what he sees: He sees his sister stripped, with her finger up her cunt, burbling laughter and wiggling her ass, a man laid out in the bedroom while she tickles the cunt to charge up another guy jerking off in the hall. He is going to spurt his orgasm on her skin, her innocent skin, her skin like living mother-of-pearl.

↣

David sits up and claps his hands to his cheeks with a slap. *Listen:* you can hear the crack of the slap. And he is making a sound. *Listen:* it is a little, light moan, as if David were groaning in his sleep.

The filthy moment has passed. Seen. Gone. In place of that picture which was so clear, David's poor mind is scattered and confused. Numb with its own violence. Numb with the bombardment about to begin.

David stands up. He walks to the workbench and stops to stare at a spot of blood that is actually there on the floor, drying. He leans on the workbench for the thousandth time. He does not look at the broken window.

He picks up the yellow-handled screwdriver. He sets it down again. He crosses the room. The scattered, outlineless images, the substanceless twinges of consciousness that had voided his awareness a moment ago, are once again beginning to congeal and take shape. David sees himself sitting on his sister and striking her. David glances down at the single spot of blood. He sees himself bashing his fist into the wall, he sees the wall beginning to cave in, he sees the wall open to him, for him. David is standing in the middle of the room, and his lips hang.

This is what he sees: Glossy pornographic pictures ripped from filthy, shiny magazines are fluttering and swirling around him like a blackening cloud of dead leaves, like locusts with their singing, devouring, electric hum, all of them descending on him, all of them rising up from his mind. Each picture

182

glistens more than the last. Asses protrude, ass holes gape, penises swell like balloons, like lungs, they grow red and they multiply, twenty, fifty, a hundred coming on like flying animals, and suddenly one small cunt is arching, like a mouth, a mouth with its invitation, a mouth with its word half-spoken. More cunts, each one wanting, each one opening, each one seeming to need something. There are twenty, fifty, some vast empty number now, of luscious little openings, wiggling, dilating, waiting at the crest of a thousand perfectly V-ing thighs and *hair! hair! hair!* Each set of red lips more slatternly and vaginal, more bee-stung. And a male thigh like iron goes soft, ripples into a pillow for sinking into, and now teats lift up their nipples as angels might lift up their adoring hands, they are aching upward now, curling up, but now they are hanging downward, hanging over him just outside his lips' reach, his lips are full, they twitch, his tongue reaches, they are hanging as fruit might hang on a tree, hanging as testicles hang.

This is what David sees: He sees a man slipping a bikini down off his butt. He sees a woman lifting and touching her own naked breasts. He sees children, vast throngs of them, crowding together, naked and squealing their arms waving, their hands feeling each other. He hears voices. He sees fists slamming. He sees bodies. He sees things. He sees things. Things.

David blinks in the sudden light from the window. His hanging lip straightens. He touches his forehead with his hand, and he closes his eyes.

Look in the window. David seems alone, bewildered in the boring room around him, silenced like a baby hearing a blasting noise. So loud that it doesn't even dare cry. David turns around and starts to walk. He stumbles over a paint can, kicks it, and keeps walking. He is pacing back and forth now, and in a minute he will go outside.

>

Look around out here. We are crossing the lawn into the green, blue, clear early-afternoon sunlight that is covering the lawn, shining everywhere now. Warm, perfect, unwavering light, more flawless than a machine. Come over to this arbor—all trees and bushes and rotting lathe and wicker—all shaded and forgotten a little bit below the garage. Step under all these green trees and feel the brightness out there grow all the more intense when seen from this shaded dark. Way to your far left is the huge fence, by the highway, looking small. To the left of that is the grove. Way up to our right is the bright-red porticoed sandstone of the house, with its big banks of windows on the second floor and the many double doorways down on the first. Directly across from us is the chalet, looking black and small. Watch.

The black door under the heavy canopy opens, and David's body, which is very far away, seems small. It stands under the massive shape a moment before the door comes closed. For an instant after it is shut, David nearly disappeared into the shadows, but now he slips out into the light, walking slowly, with his hands in his pockets again. He is ambling on the lawn, directionless, just ambling. He seems very far away. Look at his tiny feet, his white tennis shoes moving over the green.

As he walks David feels a rough hand on his neck, slapping him, forcing him down again. Grasped by the fantasy, David moves his jaw, his mouth. He violently shakes his head. He stares into the murky arbor across the way. David keeps walking on the lawn, not noticing that the brilliant green is fading away for him.

This is what David sees: He sees somebody kicking somebody very hard. He sees a bloody mouth. He sees teeth with blood on them, smeared in the spit.

David's hands are in his pockets. He is imagining something: it is Dean's face. He imagines the face, the curling smile, the dark eyes looking a little nasty. All the other images are suddenly wiped away, trash brushed aside, mere abstractions like a problem in algebra wiped away the instant a real person walks into the study and speaks. The picture is serene. David can almost feel Dean's rough-smooth cheeks.

David's walking has grown slower and more aimless. He zigzags. He seems peaceful. For the first time today everything around us seems still, and David is small and bright in his quietness, like a tiny stone undersea, under a colorless, brilliant ocean.

This is what David sees: He sees Dean in Technicolor, in a Western, and his face underneath the cowboy hat is big and laughing and very free. His arm is raised and his biceps curls, his fist grips the neck of a bottle that says "Four Roses," its label red and yellow. The brown-slatted swinging doors are standing still; there is nobody lurking behind the gleaming reddish mahogany bar, nobody has ducked to hide and the traditional saloon windows, diamond panes of green and red and white translucent glass, are unbroken. Not one captain's chair has been flung aside. All the round tables are gone. There is only one red-and-white-checked tablecloth tossed somewhere in the corner. The room is empty; there is nobody there at all; not one person crouching behind an overturned table, scared out of his mind by the shoot-'em-up. But David knows that somewhere in the room there is a woman—she is not in a Western costume, she looks like any woman—but only Dean senses her there. He can hear Dean breathing heavily through his clenched white teeth; the woman—still invisible —has pressed her fist against her cheek in terror—but no, David knows now that her hands are simply hanging at her sides, she is almost bored, and glinting almost too fast to be seen the full bottle of whiskey is once again arching downward toward the polished edge of the mahogany bar, and David hears the splintering glass and sees the pouring brown liquid spilling down over the broken glass fragments. Dean's eyes are more vicious and hard than ever, his mouth shows his uninflected hatred even more fully and utterly now than David has ever imagined it before. A large central chandelier is shining, crystal, white and candle flame. The murderous, jagged glass edges of the broken bottles gleam.

David has drifted about halfway to the green bump of the knoll, way out there to our left. He seems to be slowing down. He has just stopped walking. David drops his knees into the cushiony living grass and leans to lay his palm on it flat, testing it for wetness. The grass is dry, so he sits. David lies back and shuts out the spreading sun by closing his eyes and not thinking of anything, not seeing any pictures, his mind a gleaming, depthless, darkened void. Keeping his eyes closed, David rolls his head on the lumpy, pebbly ground, cushioned by his hair.

All pictures gone, all presences dissolved, David senses only the brilliant sun making all the light that is out there beyond his eyes. He feels only the delicious prickle of the folded blades of grass at his neck and if he opens his eyes and lifts his head he peeks down again at the scuffed white canvas shoes. David looks down there below us, lying on the ground and resting in the summer afternoon, a little slash of human color on the green.

➤

Where's Dorothy? David wonders. Wonder where she's drinking today, the bitch. These words really form and pass through his mind, though they don't provoke any decisive feeling. For a moment David sees a picture: he sees her old shaking hand gripping a tinkling glass.

With a jerk of his body, David rolls onto his stomach and his eyes open. He fingers a blade of grass, rips it loose, tickles his lips with its tip, bites it. He can see only the shapeless sunlit green around him. Except, now, for the whine.

The motorcycle engine. Dean is here finally, and he is bringing his bike around to the back of the house, moving slowly, loud and majestically as a motorboat, over the delicate little gravel path that curls around the building, toward the chalet, through hedges and bushes. He is spraying pebbles everywhere as he comes, and he leans into the slow noisy curves, turning through them with the engine shouting and barking.

David drops his head into his folded arms and turns his face away, toward the fence. He sees the fence down there. He can't be conscious of anything except that sound and he rebels against looking at Dean's majestic, glamorous arrival. David feels as if the edges of his eyelids are raw, red, he wants to sleep, his eyes have to stay closed. The revving engine hits its pitch and after a whirring squeal stops dead with a gulp. David hears Dean shifting his weight in the grotesquely big saddle; hears him lift his big body off the machine and kick down the big steel balancing rod. He can almost hear Dean's leather belt squeak.

He sits up. He turns just in time to see Dean kicking the balancing rod down with his engineer's boot. Dean is bent beside his motorcycle. He is near some bushes by the chalet. And now he turns to walk.

If you watch from here you can see both of them at once, David slim and recumbent on the grass and Dean crossing the whole field of vision from right to left, on his way to the garage. He has slipped one hand into his back pocket and his lope is chunky and graceful.

Dean notices David out of the corner of his eye and for about fifteen or twenty feet keeps him pretty clearly located there. He doesn't wave or acknowledge his presence. He is thinking. Now he looks away and forgets it.

David watches Dean from down below, enthralled with that distant animal of him walking across the landscape made by the majestic house, a loping male, its sexual flesh moving under the cloth and its dark eyes alive with their vicious indifference. Dean seems far away, like a ballet dancer moving, indifferent to the audience, behind the thick plastic sheet of the curtainline, watched like a movie of a man wiggling in outer space—though David can also imagine the naked rhythmic walking twist of Dean's black-haired abdomen. He remembers his fantasy; once again he sees the bottle in Dean's heavy hand, heavy with whiskey, slashing against the edge of the red mahogany bar, pour and leave its vicious edges gleaming. David turns away from what he sees by rolling slowly onto his side. He presses his cheek against the cool grass. It prickles his light skin, and he smells the familiar, universal green. His face is so close to the ground that the edge of his eyelid is pressed into a curling gentle blade. His two thighs are tight together, tight with the fear that makes David want to run, to jump up without caring that Dean will see, tight with the wish to run, run desperately like a wild man, not toward the house but away from it, toward the high fence. Run! Run! David is pressing his face into the grass, feeling the scrape of his bewilderment. What should he do?—not even these banal words occur to him, he only feels all that confusion infecting his senses, making the muscles themselves flaccid and feelingless. What should he do? Those words sound too much like will. He doesn't know what he will do, doesn't grasp even that he feels called upon to mobilize himself, and now that the impulse to bolt has disintegrated, he is left merely the child of his voicelessness, unable to cue even his own forehead or his own lips with a command.

David sits up. After three minutes, blind, trying to crouch himself out of existence, cringing in front of his own obscure image of what he will shortly be doing, standing in front of his adversary, wanting him while despising his superb, snotty disdain, David blinks in the sunlight, and he is touching his own knees, rubbing them a little bit. He looks up and sees across the lawn to the garage where Dean is standing in front of the electric door as it rises. David sees the grill of the limousine gleaming against its black enamel ground, ensconced in the darkness of the garage interior. Dean slips into the obscurity and disappears.

A little breeze has started up. David stands, and slipping his own hand into his back pocket begins to head for the garage.

The line between the light of the lawn and the darkness of

the garage is the line between the grassy smell of the afternoon breeze and the dark cool car stink inside, grease, road dirt, car polish, window polish, clinking steel wrenches and rubber. David's eyes immediately adjust, and standing directly in front of the black limousine he looks across the hood and sees Dean near the car stall, swabbing off a monkey wrench with an oily rag. When Dean looks up and outward at him, the secret smile is already there.

"Hey there, buddy. How's stuff, huh?" The voice is careless, bored, deep in its own confidence. David doesn't answer.

Dean shoots the rag behind him into the corner but keeps on holding the wrench.

"So what's up, man?"

"Nothing." David's voice seems to him weak and high, wavering.

There is another pause, quite a long one. "Oh yeah?" Dean says, and he flips the wrench handle in his hand. He doesn't make a single move to make himself look like he's going, even though it is obvious that his business in the garage is over, that he is about to walk out and take the wrench over to work on his bike. But he doesn't move and suddenly David is not fully aware any longer of exactly what Dean is doing or what he looks like standing there and he says instead: "Nothing new, Dean, except that I've been thinking about that stuff last night." Fool! Fool! Fool! *Thinking about that stuff last night!* Imbecile! *That stuff last night!*

There is a silence. "Well, don't." Dean's voice is curt and deep and angry. He moves the wrench in his hand again. "Because there's nothing to think about. Playing around is nothing, it's just playing around."

"Well, I think about it anyway. Because I've never done

anything like that. I mean I've never touched another person's body at all."

Dean winces. Now there's a nasty bored look on his face. "And why shouldn't I talk about it? Why shouldn't I think about it? Why not? I want to . . ."

"Look, kid—you don't know much about nothin' yet. So just remember that crap don't mean anything."

David continues to talk. "No? No? Nothing? I think it does mean something and that's all there is to it. I do think it does mean something." David's voice trembles as delicate flesh trembles when it shivers with cold. But it is getting louder.

Dean's secret smile has almost come back. He shifts his weight.

David has almost begun to focus again on the sexual animal posed in front of him, waiting in the corner.

"I'm thinking about it because I liked it. I like it. I want more of it. I want it again." The words seem out of David's mouth before they have formed in his mind, but they are all out now, tumbling. David feels amazed to find himself still standing up when he is quiet again. He presses his hands on the creased black steel of the Lincoln's hood. He looks at Dean.

"I liked it, that's all. I want it." His voice has become firm.

There is silence in the room, and now the wrench drops. Dean hooks his thumbs into his belt and leans back into the corner. His face is more deeply obscured now than ever by the shadows in the back of the stall, but David can still tell that Dean's smile is there, playing on his lips. That he is waiting.

David stands up straight and his palm prints are left as

steamy designs on the limousine's hood. David walks slowly around the car and now he reaches Dean—he is standing about three feet away. Dean has spread his legs a little more and now he folds his hands behind his back. David steps forward and makes the sudden, scary contact with real cloth, real flesh under it. He slowly pulls down Dean's fly while Dean looks up toward the ceiling, an affected expression of boredom on his face. Now he reaches forward and flips out his prick, which is big, fleshy and swelling. Dean notices David's eyes glistening like a puppy's and blinking too quickly. Dean puts out his hand and clamps it onto the boy's shoulder so that David is being forced down to his knees again.

Dean has begun to make a low sound in his throat and he is gently rolling his head as he flicks his hips to make the prick, stiff now, keep jabbing forward in provocation. David gently extends his hands and touches Dean's moving hips; he sees his own pale, boy's hands against the blue denim, moving. While he kneels, staring at Dean's penis, David imagines that he can smell something sexual, though he can't be sure, can't identify the odor. He stops; he turns the absurd thought over in his mind. The prick is bouncing stiff, jabbing toward him, but to David it seems like the detail of a picture, immobile and far away. He sees it as if it were fleshless.

"I want to see more."

"Take it, kid, suck it, suck it, take it." Dean's voice is low and self-involved in its provocative anger.

"I want to see more."

Dean grabs for the boy's shoulder, hoping to shove him further down and jerk him toward his groin, but David deftly pulls his head out of reach.

"I want to see more."

Dean's head is against the wall and his eyes are closed.

*"Take down your pants, please."

"Huh?"

"Pull down your pants."

Dean flicks his belt buckle loose and without opening his eyes, pushes down the denim and soft cotton until his entire midriff is naked.

David stares at this sexual spectacle as if the darkness which half covers it had transformed it, instead, in pale, uniform white light; as if it had all slipped behind phosphorescent glass and turned into something immaterial and merely seen. David smiles to himself as he sees the skin of the testicles moving as it adjusts to the erection; he smiles at the way the skin curls around the balls.

David sits back, rests on his heels, and puts his hands on his knees. The drowsiness and sense of indifference which had overcome him earlier return now. He again smiles to himself, almost sleepily, and quickly suppresses a decisive impulse to stand up.

"No, I won't. I don't want to." Instead of standing, he says this.

"God damn it, take it, take it, you little bastard!"

And now David does stand.

"I don't want it."

Dean's face does not register the anger which starts up in him with the immediacy of slaps on his cheek.

"Dress yourself." This command is delivered very calmly, in a voice both low and gentle.

➤

Take it easy. Lean against the closed garage door, here under the big shadow, and watch Harriet walking way out there

193

in the darkness, following her habitual path out to her lover, who as usual stays hidden in the grove until she has almost reached the knoll. Harriet's gait is firm, and the way she has her arms folded shows that she feels resolute and calm. She is walking a little faster than she was last night and the wind is blowing down on her from another direction, from behind her, circling in a vast swirl, deflected off the wide obstacle of the huge house and rolling up behind her like a wave that lifts her hair over her shoulder and blows it forward so that it streaks her cheek. She walks with the wind, in it. Ten or twelve lighted windows draw a jagged, pointed line across the house's rear façade. Look at Harriet's room at our extreme left, at the end of the second floor, the four lighted windows blazing and showing their red hopsacking curtains. Harriet has left every light in her room burning, the funnels of red light are extending from the windows as if the house were a castle undersea. The workshop chalet is dark—uninhabited and dark. Harriet has reached the knoll by now, and she is waiting—maybe she is tapping her foot—and looking around the darkness with an expression on her face that neither of us can see.

Now Harriet sees her lover coming out from the trees over there, walking toward her with his easy lope, his face strong and his eyes looking down at the ground. Harriet grips the backs of her folded arms and shivers; she scrapes her teeth together, unaware of whatever expression may be showing on her face. She doesn't take her eyes off him as he approaches. Now he has looked up and he sees her there.

➤

The man is walking across the dark grass without hurrying, confident of the way his body moves, utterly unsuspecting

194

while Harriet waits for him— Look closely at Harriet's face now—with that expression of indifference which she always has out here, the look of somebody waiting for something to be over, of somebody who keeps glancing at his watch or out the window. Perplexed a little, too—bored and perplexed. Look at Harriet's fingers moving on her arm in that nervous ripple, and notice the strange bend of her knee and the sudden but bored glance out at the highway. Harriet drops her arms and thrusts her hand forward to take his hand, the first break in the uninfracted nightly ritual. Harriet starts to talk to him, her head bent.

Walking back to the house, the two figures lean together, moving toward the backdrop of lights.

➤

Alone in his darkened bedroom (it is lit only by the light shining from his bathroom door and the thin night-light filtering in through his windows), David lies fully clothed in his bed, face down with his teeth gritting and his fists clenched. A sheet lies light across his waist and buttocks, and he feels unexpected, scary shivers jittering through his spine—and he thinks they are some kind of sex energy he can't control. David is trying to push himself into the bed. He grits his teeth and presses his face into the pillow, presses into it so hard that his lips roll apart and his teeth dry against the absorbent muslin pillowcase, tainting his lips with the taste of cloth, making them feel clean and reminding him of the hospital, of wads of cotton and the sterile feeling, even though he can smell his own sweat, his own smell, unnameable. David's feet are crossed underneath the sheet—his shoes are off—and now for a moment his waist will begin to relax a little. It seems that time has stopped moving and David is half aware of the fact that his body seemingly has begun to dissolve. He is losing himself again. David feels calm again. He holds that calm inside him the way one holds a chick still inside cupped hands—tightly and still, to make it quiet; and to keep that stillness David's outer being has to stay tight, wildly tight, and David's face in the buried pillow is a grimace of anguish, his waist snaps into mad tension again and his fists clench, clench, clench, clench, clench like a heartbeat, soothing him, reminding him of life and its peace, its softness. Time stops moving and David feels as if he's been on this bed a long time, since long before this afternoon in the garage, for instance. A fantasy, that's all, something filthy that just passed through his mind, that's all. David rolls his face in the sweaty muslin, back and forth, back and forth hard so it pulls his lips back and pinches and the pillow covers his whole face like love does. David's theatrical posture of despair is pulsating. Time keeps pressing him down, into the bed, like Dean's hand. David wants to get loose.

He rolls onto his back. He licks his lips, opens his eyes. His eyes take in the ceiling, and he rubs his palm across his forehead. He is glad to be alone. He listens, consciously, for the silence in the room, and he is reassured to find that it is still there. Lightly, absently, his hand flutters over his crotch, flutters, presses, presses, and now he again rolls over and presses his face into the pillow, and he grits his teeth again.

➤

Harriet turns from her bedroom window, where she has been standing looking out, and sees her lover, his light colored turtleneck tight around his neck, slumping in her little Chippendale chair. He looks immense to her; his sandal in the foreground is brown and huge, his thigh seems thicker than most people's waists, his face is big like something seen in a movie and the chair he is sitting in seems like a doll's chair. He is holding a little of the cloth of his trouser leg; he is pensively rolling it between his fingers as if he were testing its grain. He does not look up at Harriet, and all his dark features seem intent upon not giving her his attention. They are concentrating on the little fold of cloth, and he seems to be thinking, pondering, pouting, reflecting, considering—it is all unclear.

Harriet looks away again—she is gently pushing the red curtain to one side—and as soon as the dark lawn below her, all covered with fog, comes into focus again, Harriet tries to picture the face she has just turned away from, and she fails. His eyes. Nothing. His lips. Nothing. His torso. Nothing. Nothing. She glances hastily over her shoulder again and she sees him again, still sulking, she thinks, sulking in his perplexity, a big handsome lunk sitting in her Chippendale chair, and like a camera that snaps a picture, she turns again, carrying his image in her mind's eye. Now Harriet seems to imagine warm air moving on her neck. She imagines she can taste the tobacco on his breath.

Harriet's little hand is pressing into the hopsacking she holds, and she feels its prickles beginning to bite into her. She is imagining she can feel her lover's eyes covering her back, moving across her, devouring her, and knowing that now she has *got* to turn and say something to him; she has the folded cloth desperately in her hand, she is holding on for dear life. Harriet has *got* to speak, but she hates him, she wants him to go away, she doesn't like him, he bores her, she can't remember him, she can't remember even if he is in the room.

Now Harriet does turn and the man stands up, thinking

that the evil spell has been broken (Harriet doesn't see the relief on his face or his happy expectation). He is careful; he
doesn't want to betray his joy. He has been staring at her
haunches—he hadn't intended to, he was surprised—and
watching the curve his feelings, like liquids of need and desire,
have been spraying up through his midriff, heating him, making him want to touch, to enfold everything there that he sees.
He has been watching her little waist, and his eyes have been
damp. The fountains of feeling in him are splashing upon his
heart, making it swell up and making it start to beat loudly.

Harriet notices how quickly the man stands up. She is pain-
fully conscious of his physical weight and the presence of his
thick male body.

"My bedroom," she says with a little smile.

To her quite considerable surprise, Harriet has almost begun to cry, and she quickly turns away, looking for some gesture, some quick physical expedient that will help her forestall
this accident. She bends; she folds into the bed and her eyes,
like those of her brother, sink into the soft pillow and she sees
things now, sees them as clearly as if she were asleep, wit-
nessing a real dream.

She sees this: She sees her own body torn, her knees spread
apart and blood curling across her naked abdomen, while the
man near her laughs a vicious laugh.

She sees this: She sees him very far away, so distant that the
features of his face are wholly lost. But she can see the arms,
violent and strong. His waist is wide. He bends and lifts up a
large rock from the ground. It is heavy; he must hold it in both
hands. It is a hunk at least three feet in diameter. He throws
it to one side.

Harriet sees his elbow, his naked shoulder, very tan, just the way girls are supposed to like shoulders.

She hears this: She hears his heavy breathing. Near. Far away. Frighteningly near.

Lying on the soft bed, Harriet feels alone, alone almost to the point of being engrossed and forgetful of anyone else while she watches these pictures change. And she continues to feel alone until she feels the man's hand at her side and feels the mattress sink down when he sits down on the edge of the bed and begins to rub his hand across the backs of her legs.

Harriet doesn't yet know what to do. She must wait a little while longer without responding before she can move.

Now she turns over and looks into the man's face, which is quite close to her.

His hand is moving along her side: his eyes are full, more full than he is willing to admit or have her see, full with the water of insult and of need. His hand moves toward her waist; it creeps, like a large spider of human flesh, across the base of her abdomen and he tries to feel the skin with his fingertips, rubbing through the cloth of her skirt. It pushes into her clothes like a tiny animal; his fingers spread and he rests his hand over her crotch while his free hand begins to caress one of her breasts, gently, almost spreading a kind of love that Harriet can feel.

But Harriet turns away.

➤

David is lying on his back, both impatient with light shining in his eyes from the bathroom door and impatient with the darkness. He wants to sleep now, even though he never takes naps in the evening. And yet he can't even think of sleep. His eyes are closed but they seem to burn, and he is inflicted with the macabre sensation of eyeballs against eyelid skin, and his legs are jumpy. He jerks his head on the pillow and the movement suddenly makes him aware that his back is much too rigid for sleep, that it is stiff with terror. With an effort of will, David tries to make his back relax; his mind delivers the command. He thrashes back and forth seven times in the bed, holding his pillow against the back of his head with his uplifted arms, counting each tossing spasm—one, two, three—all to the sound of the cloth and mattressing being thrashed and flounced, getting sweaty, filthy. But now David is still, sinking into the bed again while his feelings scatter and shoot through his limbs, painful, vague, unnamed.

➤

She is lightly fingering the cloth on her sleeve, but she keeps gently watching the man, not afraid to look at him, the way she was a few minutes ago. She notices that he is pacing.

➤

Step out from behind these trees. Look up at Harriet's bedroom—there where the four windows with red hopsacking curtains are blazing away. Both of them are in there. If you watch closely even from here you'll be able to see her lover pacing back and forth in front of the windows. There—there he goes, past the third window over. There! But now he's gone.

➤

The man moves past the bed again still talking and Harriet follows him with her eyes. This time he's really mad. Notice his face, how red and violent it is. Harriet takes in the lush knit fabric of his turtleneck pullover—it looks terribly expensive and it covers his big upper torso with a kind of gentle pastel floss. He has pulled up the sleeves as if in exasperation and Harriet is suddenly very conscious that his biceps curve just the way she has been told women are supposed to like men's biceps, and she particularly notices a big vein crossing the left one. Lots of women would like him—Harriet glances over him again—*lots* would, she supposes.

And now Harriet maintains a serious expression while she begins to smile inside—she can almost hear herself laughing in there, clapping her hand over her mouth and giggling a girlish sixteen-year-old guffaw—and she recedes from him, from his hulky, straining, present body, from his anger, and his words which she had noticed were so very loud, which were like pistol shots, but which she can't hear very well now. . . .

Harriet's eyes still rest on him and his pacing anger, but he doesn't know that he has been left alone.

Now he's bending over her, his fist has been raised up tight near his own chin, and he's shouting, *"Listen to me, you little bitch! At least listen!"*

Harriet doesn't reply, and her lover's face all distorted with feeling as it leans so close to hers—it is less than a foot away—seems to her to sink back into space, receding almost beyond the wall opposite her bed. She watches him the way a forest ranger might watch an animal passing unaware beneath the watchtower, thinking itself all alone, unaware that it is prowling at the base of a man-made structure. From behind the glass panels that slide so neatly across the lookout platform, Harriet can stare down at the human beast below and she sees that the thing is wounded, moving spastically in its pain. It howls, it makes a sound that rings through the entire forest with a cry intended to penetrate every space to the depths, intended to warn everyone, notify everything, the cry is a path out of desperation because the animal is alone and afraid, afraid it is going to die and the terror of death is moving through its consciousness now, at this very moment. The animal screams simultaneously for, of, and from solitude, and watching from above, Harriet notes that solitude has made the poor thing even more bestial.

"Why, why? Why the fuck did you have to make me come up here at all?" The man's face is now so close that Harriet can see his pupils dilate and make out the splayed webby red veins in the corners of his eyes.

Harriet doesn't need even to remind herself that she is watching the end of an affair that has already been terminated. It is like watching a poorly made kinescope re-run of a play that has already closed. She sees her lover's face in black and white and for the moment the sound in the machine has gone off, though he is still talking to her. He has interesting, pretty lips. Harriet's face betrays no expression whatever. Her eyes lift calmly to meet his when he comes near. She follows his movement in the room, indifferent to whether he is far away or close.

"Well, you could at least say something, you know! I know you're just a kid, but you are also responsible, aren't you? Isn't that what you want? Isn't it? You could at least try to be. . . ."

Again Harriet does not reply. The person in this room is already gone.

"What did I do? Just tell me that, Harriet . . . what did I do?"

Harriet's neck feels a little cramped on the pillow and she wonders if she dares move. She decides that she does not.

The empty eye continues to gaze, scarcely blinking, and one corner of her mouth moves out of nervousness and tension into what the bewildered man opposite her imagines is a smile.

Look at the windows and the lights still extending their beams from them, now spreading into funnels that look like searchlights shining, from a bathysphere undersea.

➤

"It gives you a kick, doesn't it? That's why! That's why! It's just kicky for you to turn into ice like this, isn't it?"

Harriet can hardly hear his words, but still they very gently touch the far edge of her perception, brush against it, leave a little trail of meaning which begins to glow and is slowly assimilated though she hears the words moving inward from that edge the way one hears a radio playing two floors down or the way sound passes through a viscous medium so that the soft, gentle sound breaks on the ear a long time after the distant lips start screaming. Harriet gets the accusation. She wants to reply, but she hasn't yet amplified the words sufficiently to hear them. Straining her attention and blocking out everything else, she has to play them over and over again before they come clear and she really knows what has been said to her.

Now Harriet replies, her empty eyes filling a little. "No," she says. "No, it's not. No, it's not." She is whispering, hardly audible, she scarcely hears her own words, he can't hear her, only we can hear her if we strain. . . . "No. No. No, it's not," she says.

Her reply almost expresses her abashment. The thin movement of her voice is almost provoked by the hint of decency. But all that dies away.

"No. That's not true," and her voice is as empty as the taped articulations of a computer with a voice taped into the works.

"Then you're afraid! You're afraid of me!"

He draws even more close to her.

"You brought me up here because you're afraid. You want to kick me out but you're afraid to do it; you think I won't take it and that I won't let you do it. Believe me, Harriet, I'll let you do it. You've got nothing to worry about; it's an easy matter to walk out on you. But why are you so scared? Admit it! What scares you? *What scares you? Do you think I'm going to do something to you, think I'm going to hurt you? Is that it? Is that what you think I'm going to do?"*

Harriet moves her mouth in a gesture of mere negativity. Her eyes blink their vapid refusal. She does not even consider the justice of what has been said, does not even acknowledge that someone has spoken.

"All right then, I'll leave. That's easy. I'll just leave, simple as that."

He has moved away from her, walking slowly backward, and as he draws away the feelings that have been twisting his face subside and leave his olive skin smooth.

"You think I need you?"

Only more silence.

"You think . . ."

The man remembers very well that he had brought nothing with him, and so he doesn't even cast a hasty glance around the room, and walks to the door.

>

The hallway outside Harriet's bedroom is unfamiliar, long, and incredibly old-fashioned, like somebody's grandmother's

204

house, but bigger than anybody ever dreamed of, naturally. The man who has just closed the bedroom door without taking any precaution about the noise is untroubled by the possibility that somebody might spot him as he walks to the narrow servant's staircase by which Harriet brought him upstairs. He does not leave by the main staircase. *Come with me to the head of the big stairway and look down.*

>—

David is sitting at the foot of the stairs, with his head down, resting it on his arms. Now he lifts his head and peers again through the open door of Dorothy's sitting room where she is sitting drinking right now. Looking from this angle, the boy can't see anything except some flowered chintz upholstery over a couch and the only thing he can hear is the sound of the television set, which is itself very indistinct. Once in a while it is interrupted by Dorothy's voice cackling. She is speaking words he can't understand.

Now David stands up and walks into the center of the large entry hall at the base of the stairs. Now he can really see her. She sits, sunk in a deep armchair, her drink in her left hand, wrapped up in the image on the television screen, and for the moment, silent. Though she is perfectly plain to David, it is very unlikely that Dorothy is going to notice him. David's hands hang loose and graceless at his sides. He stands still to watch.

This is what he sees: The woman's arm is bent peculiarly, and she has picked up her drink in an equally strange way, with her wrist twisted back in an unusually stiff, awkward position. Her head is rocking back and forth on the cushions of the chair, she makes a sound like that of someone humming tune-lessly, or a woman speaking without words.

David moves away in an arc still farther from the staircase and now he can quite clearly make out Dorothy's profile. Her lips are moving. She has plastered her tongue over her lower lip and she is sucking at them both.

This is what David sees: He sees a woman bewildered by the drinking that is now the only activity in her life; he sees her imagining two men and their violence. One of them rocks on his naked buttocks; the corners of his mouth are very wet; his penis, still perfectly erect, bounces a little when he walks. The other man is entirely different. He is old-fashioned; he is adjusting his necktie. His mouth is a straight, fleshless line under a glossy mustache.

Dorothy lifts her drink again and tries to look through the glass and liquid at the light of the television screen. Naturally she can't, so she takes a slug and then slurps at the glass again, with a hiss.

Dorothy is muttering to herself again, and now her right hand, the free one, begins to fondle her breast. She is saying something she alone can understand, and now she sets her drink safely on a side table, so that both hands are free. She wipes her right hand across her eyes. Again she stares at the flickering screen, trying to understand what she has lost since the last time she understood the plot or what was going on. Now she's making something out: she sees a woman's face, and on the black-and-white television screen the woman's per-fectly shaped lips appear to be black. The woman's hand is moving very little. (Dorothy doesn't understand what she is saying.) She smiles with her black lips.

Dorothy is trying to smile, too, smile in the same way, but she can't quite make the grade. Her lips, numb with the chemical, won't move that way. She is particularly conscious that her lips are not firm like the black ones, but flabby, and she knows that her smile is ugly. To make her lips as firm as the ones she sees she must stretch her lips across her teeth. Her face becomes a hideous grimace.

Dorothy again sinks into her chair. Again she rolls her head on the cushions behind her neck. Now she says some very obscene words very sharply, very loudly. It seems loud even to David out in the foyer, and it makes him jump.

�

David feels as if he were standing in an open field alone. He watches the woman's head rolling; he sees that her eyes are closed, and that so far from having the perfect artificial coloring implied by the face both she and David have just seen on the screen, Dorothy's face has taken on the white, void pallor cast by the electric tube.

David returns to the base of the stairs and sits again, lowering his head once more. Stand here at the top of the stairs and look down on his bent back. His heavy breathing is making it expand, expand like the chest of a man who is sleeping deeply. David lifts his head again and presses his face into his palm. Now he twists his body around so that he is almost facing us. He has made a firm fist; he is pressing it down on the carpet of the stair directly above him. Now he is looking up toward us, and the expression in his eyes is one that we have not noticed before.

✳

Now he is standing still in the empty room. Now he rests against the window sill. He remains perfectly quiet and he seems to be listening for any sound that might betray anyone's approach. He has lifted his hands to his own rib cage, and he presses them against it, feeling the warmth of his palms. His fingers move like tentacles across his own face, and give the impression of moths fluttering in the darkness against his skin. With his fingertips, he is testing the curve of his cheek. He feels the pure, clear bend of his forehead. His hands run up and down the fronts of his thighs, so often and so roughly that they grow hot with the friction. He squeezes his left knee.

David stands again. Now he sits. He rests. He closes his eyes. He listens.

✈

Harriet steps into the darkened hallway outside her bedroom, and very, very slowly begins to walk toward the little staircase that leads to the third floor. She is tiptoeing. The carpet is very deep.

Inside Harriet's empty bedroom, every light has been turned out. All you can see are four big panes of whitish black, fogged opacity at the windows. Come to the windows. Try to look out. The fog is everywhere, everything is gone. You can't see the grove, not even its outline, not even the shape of a single tree. The fence, the lights on the highway, both have become invisible, been covered in impenetrability. The black chalet is gone. The garage is gone. The grass, the knoll, the arbor, the yard. Everything is gone.

Turn around and come, step back into the hall. Harriet has almost reached the staircase door. She is still very slowly tiptoeing, with her back turned toward us. Now she reaches it and stops. Her hands hang loose; she seems at a loss, trying to decide what to do. She turns now; she leans her back against the door frame of the narrow set of stairs. She draws her right hand through her hair, jerking at the strands so hard that her scalp is pulled tight and the corners of her mouth are drawn up, and her eyes are mock-Chinese. Now she lets it all go and shakes her head, trying to shake her hair back into place, blowing some air through her nose and moving her head again, roughly, as if she wanted to shake some nasty, bitter taste from her mouth.

She leans again, but this time her eyes are closed and their line is serene. Now she opens her eyes again, turns, and reaches with her right hand into the darkness, feeling for the banister, and now she pulls at it and begins to climb.

We are standing at the top of the third-floor staircase. Now you are going to hear Harriet's footsteps and in a moment she will stumble and lose her balance a little at the top. There she is. She kneels into our field of vision and appears. Blackness.

Harriet stands up straight again. She isn't wearing any shoes. The hallway is completely dark.

Harriet turns her head back and forth, trying to look from one end of the hallway to the other even though she can't see a thing anywhere. She can't remember if she is supposed to turn left or right. She can't remember what the doorway looks like, even though she can't see it anyway. She turns to her right and crosses the hall. Listen. Now she has reached a closed door over there. She turns the door knob, swings it open. Things are still.

Harriet has lost her bearings in the darkness and she decides to come back to the head of the little staircase. A little bit of light is shining up through it from the second floor and she can see her way back easily, without having to test her steps before she takes them or extend her arms in front of her like a blind woman, groping. But still she walks back slowly, as if she were walking along the face of a cliff, on an unsteady ledge, and when she reaches the head of the stairs again she turns and stands still a long time, feeling safe at last, breathing heavily in relief. Listen. There isn't any sound anywhere except her breathing. Listen to it. Harriet herself can't hear anything except her own breath now. She holds her breath and strains to hear. Silence. She is waiting, waiting to remember something, to see it. Waiting to see the lawn maybe, spread beneath her like a bed. Waiting to see the little boy in short pants grumpily climbing up the narrow staircase that tumbles down behind her now. Harriet holds her breath again. Maybe she is remembering the heavy body she has just banished.

Stand back. Harriet has begun to move again; she has stepped into the darkness and the feeble light from the stairs doesn't illuminate her any more. She is walking to her left, the correct way this time, cautiously feeling out each step in the darkness. Her arms extend lightly in front of her. Wait. Listen to that—the sound of her hands feeling on wood. The door frame. Now she is fumbling at the door, feeling with spread fingers inside it, against the wall, trying to find the light switch, and she tries both sides—listen to her body moving from one side to the other—and now she touches the light switch, starting as if she had accidentally touched a living animal, a mouse. She cups it in her hand and freezes. On second thought, she decides not to turn it on.

Cautiously, cautiously, testing the space in front of her with outstretched hands, Harriet takes two steps into the darkness.

Step in behind her, even though you can't see. Stand in the doorway. Wait.

All that we can hear are the imperceptible movements of Harriet's body and the tiny sound of her naked feet padding very slowly on the floor. After three steps she stops dead still and extends her right arm in a broad arc about her, moving it the way a lighthouse beam sweeps a seascape. But she doesn't touch a thing. Now she takes three more steps, but with the second step her bare sole comes down on the sharp pointy plastic bodies of three toy soldiers bristling with rifles and flame throwers and hand grenades. She winces and brushes them all away with a sweeping movement of her foot. Listen to the mouselike little plastic clatter. Harriet takes a fourth step, a fifth, a sixth. Each is more confident. Again she stops and swings her arms around her like the double beams of a searchlight moving across the black sky, parallel to the horizon. But once again nothing obstructs their path. Harriet decides not to walk any farther. She speaks instead.

"Davy." It is a whisper, a whisper. It can scarcely be heard. We can hardly hear it. Harriet stands still.

Again, her arms very slowly test their arc around her, testing, touching nothing. Again she drops them to her side.

"Davy," she says once more, loudly enough this time for all of us in the room to hear her. But there isn't any answer. Silence.

Harriet is standing motionless in front of us, straining, trying to silence every sense except her ears. And there! There! Listen. I heard some movement. I hear it. Listen.

Harriet shifts her weight, and now stands still again.

"*Davy!*" The whisper is loud and urgent.

"Davy." It is inaudible. We can't hear it at all.

Harriet's arm tests the arc again, moving very slowly, moving with both hands, with her fingers sensitive and extended. She touches nothing. The room is absolutely black. Harriet takes two more steps and once again her bare foot comes

211

down on a plastic soldier. She winces and brushes it away. *"Davy!"*

She repeats the searching movement with her hands again, and this time David's wrist stops the slow arc of her right arm. His hand closes around her wrist. Her wrist feels very thin and weak. Harriet lowers her hands.

"Davy!"

David doesn't release her wrist from his gentle grip. He draws her nearer and he whispers, "Harriet . . ." Stop. Listen to them. "Harriet, I've been waiting . . ." he says. Now he takes her other hand. Peer into the darkness, you won't see a thing. Now Harriet lifts her released left hand and to her small surprise she touches David's chest and then lets her hand slide downward until she is touching his side, until her fingers are feeling his breathing side, his waist. Both David's hands are moving upward—now he is cupping her cheeks in his palms. Harriet's right hand lifts and her fingertips touch David's still lips. Now David's arms are around her, on her shoulders, and her hands are touching her brother's back, moving gently up and down. Listen. You can hear only the sound of them moving. Nothing else. The room is entirely dark. Harriet's hands still caress up and down, cool against the cloth, against the flesh of David's back, and David's fingers are touching Harriet's shoulder blades, touching them, and both are touching now, both being touched—her back, his lips, her eyes, his eyes, his lips, her thigh, his back, his abdomen, her buttocks, his lips, her lips, his forehead, her hips, her . . . him . . . her . . . his . . . she . . . he.

212